CW01648746

THE VALLEY OF BICHO

R.F. BLACKSTONE

SEVERED PRESS
HOBART TASMANIA

THE VALLEY OF BICHO

WWW.SEVEREDPRESS.COM

ISBN: 978-1-922551-57-3

For Tyrion Rottweiler Pug Paddon, a more loyal friend, brother and companion there ever was. He shall meet us in Valhalla.

CHAPTER ONE

"You took your time," General Carpenter said, not bothering to look up at the man who seconds before had walked into the makeshift office.

Major Henry Armitage wiped the sweat from his brow as his eyes took in the tent's interior. Just like the General's proper office, this was spartan. Built for use and not for comfort. A small table, two chairs, a corkboard with mission details and a mini-fridge decorated the space. "Sorry Sir," Armitage's voice was soft but with an edge to it, "had some trouble getting a transport run here."

Carpenter waved the excuse away. "Details, details, details," he said, "spare me the details and just get fucking on with it." His clear blue eyes found Armitage, and the older man's mouth split open in a wide grin. "But damn if you aren't a sight for sore eyes!"

At the welcoming tone, Armitage's face too broke out in a smile and the men clasped hands tightly. "Been far too long, Sir," he agreed before releasing the General's hand.

"True, but I don't want you to wear out your welcome," Carpenter said with a laugh. A wrinkled, shaking hand wiped his brow, and the man muttered, "I hate this fucking weather."

Armitage suppressed a chuckle. He had to admit it. The heat

mixed with the Mexican humidity made every movement seem heavier and slower. The Major was used to it though, he'd been on missions before in the country with his team and had developed a strange taste for it. Armitage blamed the soft-drink called Yoli for that. At the thought of an icy-cold soda, saliva filled his mouth, and the man said, "Any chance for a drink, Sir?"

Carpenter didn't hear him. Fixing his eyes on a spot outside the tent, he focused and unfocused them, trying to see something of importance. "Did you bring all of them?" he asked after what seemed like an eternity of silence.

Armitage turned and saw what the General was looking at.

On the far side of the camp, a Sikorsky UH-60 Black Hawk sat waiting patiently as the sun rose behind it. The propellers spun as the motor wound down and the dust settled around the blades' perimeter. From out of the helicopter's side, five men clambered down with no problems. Their movements were precise and came from muscle memory. Each one carried a duffel bag and moved with the measured steps of professional killers.

Armitage smiled with pride at his team. "Of course, Sir," he said as the two continued to watch the team, known as The Cutthroats, go about stowing their gear and relaxing. "You told me the mission needed the best."

Carpenter's eyes narrowed slightly. "True," he said, "but I thought the team was bigger?"

"It used to be," Armitage said after a brief pause. "The last mission, Siberia, took some heavy casualties."

"Sorry for the loss," the General said. He sniffed, cracked his knuckles, then cleared his throat before saying, "It looks like you have the essentials there."

Armitage watched as the old man went over to the small table and picked up a handful of folders. Each one had the symbol of the Cutthroats on it: a skull with two cutthroat razors crossing each other on the diagonal making the crossbones. Carpenter glanced at each folder, reading out loud the name on it, "Carter. Gilman. Muldoon. Nightingale. Ward. All good men and trustworthy to boot."

"If they weren't," Armitage answered, "they wouldn't be out there."

The General laughed at the bluntness of the younger man's answer. That was the thing about Henry Armitage, he always spoke his mind and it made working with him much easier. "Good," the old man said. "You'll want men like that with you at all times. And this situation will prove it perfectly."

"And what is the situation, Sir?"

Carpenter shook his head, "In a word? FUBAR."

Armitage's eyes widened slightly. In all his years working for the General he had never heard him use any of the acronym's usually used by the military. "That bad?"

"In a word, again. Yes," Carpenter nodded, then motioned with his head for Armitage to check out the board. "All the pertinent intel is there. But, trust me Hank, you won't like it."

"Let me be the judge of that," Armitage said as his eyes went over the pinned pieces of paper. Tacked to the cork was a dossier of a man, blueprints of a large fortified compound and a map of the local terrain and area. Dense jungle surrounded the target's location which when combined with the humidity and heat of the Mexican summer, spelled one thing. "Fucking hell!"

"Thought you'd like it."

Armitage's eyes went back to the dossier, "Who's the target?"

"A real villain if ever there was one. Makes Guzman, Escobar and Blanco look like school children. The higher-ups want him something fierce." The older man pointed to the official-looking photo of the target, "His name is Jorge Galindo, but the locals call him 'El Dandy'."

"The Dandy?" Armitage snorted as his eyes studied the dossier.

The black and white mug shot stapled to the dossier showed a man who knew his worth and what the world owed him. Big brown eyes that looked kind stared at the man, wire-rimmed glasses hid the cunning and cruelty that hid behind the kindness. Even though it was obvious Galindo had the shit kicked out of him before they took the photo, the smile the man wore reminded Armitage of a politician. "Seems like a lovely guy."

"Makes Mother Teresa look like a whore," Carpenter laughed as he handed his friend a tall bottle of water. "Trust me, you'll need to stay hydrated for this one."

Armitage took a long pull on the bottle and relished the icy feeling of the water running down his throat. "So, basically," he said, "this is a snatch and grab. Release after?"

"Most likely not. He's going to be enjoying the hospitality of the finest facilities we can offer," Carpenter said with a wolfish smile. The man drifted to the map of the compound. "The foliage is too thick for us to get better images, but thermal gave us the basic layout. Sorry, Hank, but you'll be going in blind."

Armitage shrugged. He'd been in worse conditions and came out the other end with barely a graze. "It's my job to do the impossible. But, Sir, a question."

Carpenter's raised eyebrow gave him all the permission he needed.

"Why us?"

"Because I need the best," Carpenter said, and his tone of voice made Armitage pause. There was a tiny shake to it that the other man had never heard before.

"Sir," Armitage started making sure his voice was filled with calm and serenity, "no disrespect meant. But, you've got access to other teams who are more suited for this type of work. The Cutthroats are not delivery boys."

"Today you are," the General snapped. His eyes flashed with an anger that just as quickly vanished. "Sorry Hank," he mumbled as he slid into his seat. "This one came out of the blue, hence the rush to get a team here."

Armitage crossed his arms. "You know I hate rush jobs, Sir," he said. "If I run this past the boys and they say no, you're up shit creek—"

"Then don't run it past them," Carpenter said. He smiled at his friend and his voice became calm. "Look at it like this. What the boys don't know, can't hurt them, right?" His smile seemed slightly forced, and that made Armitage even more suspicious.

"Right," the other man said before putting the bottle down on the table. "But bullets, knives, and fuck knows what else is out there can."

"You sound like a mother," the General laughed as he went back to the table. With a groan he sat, reached under the top and pulled out a pack of cigarettes. "Your boys can handle themselves better than any others I know." He offered the skeptical man a smoke.

Armitage shook his head. "This stinks, Sir," he said. It was true, and both men knew it. Unfortunately, that was the nature of the beast.

"It's the way of the world," Carpenter said, as if he was reading Armitage's thoughts. "You know it, Hank. I get my orders, which then goes to you. Shit always runs downhill, never up."

"Always the philosopher," Armitage said with a slight shake of his head. No matter what happened, he knew he could always count on his friend and commanding officer. "At least give me more than this," he said with a dismissive wave of his hand.

Carpenter looked at their surroundings. Outside the tent, the hustle and bustle of combined forces reminded him of ants. His trained ears focused on the different languages mingling together, English and Spanish being thrown about as the local officials tried to take control of the situation. The desperation in their voices brought a smile to the old face.

"Sir?" Armitage's voice snapped the General out of his reverie and the man looked up from his seat.

"Sit down, Hank. You're making the place untidy."

Dutifully, Armitage sat on a fold-out chair that groaned and threatened to break under his weight. "Sir," he said again, "you've got to give me more than this clandestine bullshit."

Nodding along, Carpenter agreed with his friend. "There isn't much," he said with a slight cough. "Just that the Mexicans needed help getting through the rat's nest. According to them, they don't have any teams good enough to grab Galindo."

Neither man believed this, but they were in no position to contradict the Mexican Government. All Armitage did to show his opinion was to grunt and fold his arms.

"My feelings exactly," Carpenter said before wiping his brow. The sheer amount of sweat that stained it darkened the military green shirt, and the man looked at it in disgust. "Fuck me, I forgot how hot it was here."

"Maybe the General needs a refreshing beverage?" Armitage offered helpfully.

Carpenter laughed as he reached under the table. He groaned

from the strain on his old muscles and said, "This is definitely a young man's game. Being out in the field is no place for a distinguished gent like me." With another groan, he sat upright and placed a bottle of scotch on the table. In his other hand, he held two glasses.

Ignoring the opportunity to poke fun at his commanding officer, Armitage said, "Don't change the subject, Sir. What's really going on?"

His eyes watched as Carpenter poured the golden liquid into the glasses, then casually slid one towards Armitage. They raised the glasses in a silent toast, then sipped, enjoying the burn and warmth as the liquid travelled down their throats.

"Remember all the trouble we had with bin Laden? There are some who think that eventually, Galindo will grow as powerful and nobody will be able to stop him. We're just getting ahead of a problem," Carpenter said, then finished his drink in one gulp.

"He's just another Mexican drug lord. Doesn't seem special to me."

The knowing laugh from the Colonel sent a chill down the team leader's spine. "Then what's the problem?" Carpenter asked with another chuckle. "If he's not special, then it should be a walk in the park. Right?"

Glancing at the corkboard, Armitage nodded silently to himself. The mission would a challenge solely because of the terrain and lack of intel. Other than that, it appeared to be a run-of-the-mill job. There was no real reason for him not to take it. "What about the area?" Armitage asked, pointing to the map of the area. "Looks like nothing but jungle."

"We don't really have much intel about the area," Carpenter said while rubbing his neck. "The locals call it 'The Valley of Bicho', and from what I can tell, the real reason they came to us is because they aren't stupid enough to go in there."

Armitage turned slowly to his old friend and spoke, "Superstitions? Tell me I'm not going to be sweating my ass in the middle of the jungle because they won't go in?" He laughed harshly, "Fucking hell, General! Is this some kind of sick joke?"

The air hung with tension as the General took in the man's words. Armitage stared at him, then to the map of the area. Of course the mission was rotten, but there was nothing either man could do. The only thing he could do was smile pleasantly at the Major.

"Would it help," Carpenter said while refilling his glass, "if I gave you a direct order?"

CHAPTER TWO

The Black Hawk helicopter rose high into the air, and waited a second before flying back to the makeshift base-camp on the shore of the sun-swept beach. As it vanished from sight, the six-man team known as The Cutthroats casually checked their gear.

"We good?" Armitage's voice was soft but came through crystal clear across their comms.

Randolph Carter gave a quick thumbs-up, then instantly wiped the sweat from his bald head. Glancing up at the noon sun, the second-in-command squinted then muttered, "Should've brought fucking sun-screen."

The other five men shook their heads and chuckled at the man's fretting over his scalp. The largest of the team, Sam Nightingale, walked over to his friend. His hulking form pushed the grass and branches aside, and he loomed over the smaller man. Without a word, his hand dove into a side pocket of his pack and pulled out a small green flat cap.

"Bring enough for the rest of us?" Walter Gilman asked as Carter inspected the cap before lacing atop his head with a satisfied sigh.

Nightingale turned and blew a kiss while giving the man the finger. This brought another round of laughter from the team. This was all part of the routine before any mission started.

"Cut the shit," Armitage said as he adjusted his own pack, shifting the weight so it sat perfectly on his back.

"Kinda tense, ain't we boss?" Tommy Muldoon said as he played with a straight razor. The sharp blade glinted in the harsh sunlight and the bright reflection bounced off his sunglasses. "Wanna be careful with that. Stress is the number one killer out there."

"Is. That. A. Fact?" Armitage asked while giving the man the greatest deadpan stare of all time. Even though he stood shorter than any of the others on his team, Henry Armitage was more intimidating and imposing than any of them. "You done playing with your cock?"

His deadly serious tone mixed with the question got a round of laughs from the rest of the men. Only Muldoon remained silent. He fumbled with the razor, trying to flip it closed with one hand. Each attempt was a failure, and soon he'd hurt himself.

"Can we get a wriggle on, gentlemen?" Carter asked as he checked their co-ordinates. "Daylight's fading fast and I've had enough of burning my ass off."

"Sir!" the three men sounded off as one unit and it brought a smile to Armitage's face.

"Let's move out," he ordered, then turned and trudged into the dense foliage of the Lacandon Jungle. As he walked, he said, "Sam. Take point. Disney, join him."

The team watched as both Gilman and Nightingale jogged ahead of the team. They held their M4A1 carbine rifles tightly to their chests, their fingers resting on the trigger guard, slowed and scanned the trees and bushes.

"I hate when you call me that," Gilman said with an annoyed grunt. "It's Walter."

Carter laughed then said, "But we love your movies so much, Disney. I can't wait for the next live action remake."

The point-man went silent as they continued walking through the jungle. They took each step with precision and care as they ducked under low-hanging branches and cut down thick vines. And even though they weren't that long into the mission, the six men were already drenched in sweat.

"Why the fuck are we here again, Sir?" Charles Dexter Ward said as he used a large green leaf to wipe the salty-liquid from his face. "Dammit, why couldn't this be somewhere cool?"

"You'd rather be back in Siberia?" Armitage asked without looking at the team's medical officer. His eyes darted about the greenery and his muscles were already tense. He was ready for anything, even though he moved casually.

At the mention of Siberia, the others became serious and quiet. The only sounds to come from the six men were the heavy boots crushing dead pieces of foliage, their rifles and sidearms clicking with each step. It provided a strange musical accompaniment to the natural sounds of the jungle; the creaking of the trees in the breeze, birds singing and in the distance, the faint hooting of monkeys.

"Why you gotta go there?" Muldoon said as he fiddled with the zipper of his vest.

Nightingale's voice rumbled as he said, "To stop Disney from crying about those remakes."

"Will you stop calling me that?!" Gilman's voice cracked from the frustration he felt. Ever since he joined the team, that was the name the Major had given him, and every single man in the team now called him that. "My fucking name is—"

"—Walt Disney," Carter said with a raucous laugh that echoed through the jungle.

"Keep it down!" Armitage barked. "There's no telling who is out there. We can't afford to give our position away. Understand?"

His men nodded, then a second later the second-in-command said, "Hank, what is out there?" It was an innocent enough question, but the fact he asked it sent a ripple of doubt through the others. Sensing this, Carter followed his question with, "What's the target?"

"Some cartel-boss," Armitage said, and his voice filled with annoyance. "We need to take out his men, grab him, then get to the pickup. All in the same day."

"A fucking delivery deal," Muldoon said what the others were thinking. "I'm sweating my ass off in the middle of bum-fuck to be a delivery boy?"

"We," Nightingale corrected. "We're sweating our collective

asses off."

"There has to be more to this," Carter said, and his voice was suspicious. Armitage never took on a job without knowing every single detail. "Spill the beans, boss."

Armitage slowed, his face set in a blank expression that worried his friend. "That's it," he said. "Get in. Grab the package. Get out."

"Bada bing, bada bang," Gilman said with a chuckle. "At least we won't run into anything like in Siberia."

"Don't you mention that place again," Muldoon said with a shudder. "I never want to see a bear again in my entire life!"

The men laughed, each one pushing down the feeling of loss and pain from the mission. Instead, they focused on Muldoon's moment of constant suffering. "Still don't know why you didn't want to be his cub?" Armitage asked and his question sent the men into fits of silent laughter.

"Keep it down," Carter said, doing his best at sounding like his friend. "We don't know what's out there, remember?"

The men continued to laugh as they went further and further into the Lacandon Jungle. Even with the humidity and consistent sweating, the way the rays of sunlight broke through the canopy was beautiful. Henry Armitage looked at the bright greens and smiled. This was part of the job he enjoyed, the different locations and sights they got to see. The only downside he saw was that they never got to enjoy them properly; he'd love to have a proper vacation in Cancun or Playa del Carmen.

"Boss? Boss, don't go into the light. It's a trap," Ward's voice was distant, but the joke made the Major blink.

"Sorry," Armitage said with a small smile. "What were we talking about?"

Nightingale's voice came through the comms, "How our dear brother, Tommy, almost became the lover of a big bear."

"Shut up, will ya!"

Gilman laughed and ducked under a tree branch. "It's not fun when it's you on the receiving end," he said.

"What's that, Disney?" Muldoon shot back instantly. "You're going to remake Robin Hood, and this time you're making it an all-female cast? Very transgressive and woke."

The moment the man uttered the word Disney, Walter Gilman's mouth clamped shut. He turned his focus on monitoring the way ahead and making sure his brothers-in-arms weren't walking into a trap.

"Don't take it to heart," Nightingale said, having switched the comms channel, so it was just the two of them. "They only do it because they care."

Gilman shook his head. "The reason doesn't matter," he said before lifting his rifle and peering through the attached scope. He stopped moving and raised his hand.

Behind them the four men stopped and crouched down, making sure they weren't visible to anyone with thoughts of violence. The giant next to him also brought his gun up and looked through the scope. His finger twisted the focus knob on the top of it, and slowly the blurry image became sharp and clear. "What am I looking for?"

"What's the problem?" Carter's voice was low and hushed through the comms. "Disney, what d'you see?"

Nightingale stared at his brother in arms then scanned the area. He couldn't see anything except the trees, vines and large ferns. Glancing back to Walter Gilman, the man knew that he hated the nickname. Something shifted slightly a few meters ahead of them and he finally found what had alarmed the other man. It was a snake, slithering through the trees. "Nothing," Nightingale said after a second of silence.

"Just local wildlife," Gilman added quickly. "Sorry, boss. Won't happen again."

"No worries," Armitage said. He didn't sound upset or annoyed. "Better safe than sorry, right?"

"Yeah," Muldoon said. "Outstanding work, Disney."

"Nicely done, Rosie," Ward added with a small chuckle.

Gilman groaned and started walking again. "Thanks," he said with a tone of absolute resignation to the nickname. The others heard it and laughed.

"Boss," Nightingale said as they continued moving through the jungle, "What is it about this place the locals don't like?" Always the scientific mind, Sam Nightingale spoke little and only read.

Armitage ducked under a branch and spotted a colourful frog staring at him. It was bright red and green; the colours were beautiful, but he knew better than to touch it. “No idea. All I was told was that the locals fear this place. Which is why I want you all on guard. No visits from Mister Cock-up.”

“And what if we run into any villains?” Ward asked as he shifted the position of the rifle’s strap.

“I expect nothing less than gratuitous violence from the lot of you,” Armitage said with a big smile. His eyes went across each man in his team and an overwhelming sense of pride went through him. “Remember, you keep the fire down. You get stuck in and you kick their fucking teeth out, or I guarantee you, I fucking guarantee you, they will eat your balls for brekkie. And yes, I mean you, Tommy.”

Muldoon turned and looked shocked to be singled out. “Is that because of Siberia? I’m shocked. Shocked with the lot of you.”

“No,” Carter said, barely containing his laughter. “He’s referring to New Orleans.”

As the members of The Cutthroats laughed, their voices coming together as one. Tommy Muldoon took a moment to think, then nodded. “Yeah, fair call.”

Armitage’s head went up and his nose twitched. He wasn’t one hundred percent sure what the strange smell was that assaulted his nostrils; it might’ve been the fresh air mixed with shit and the marijuana plants littering the jungle. Then again, there was a distinct flavour filling his mouth that could’ve only been one thing.

Death.

“Cut the shit,” he said as his thumb flipped the rifle’s safety to off. “Eyes open, mouths closed. Now.”

Without argument, the five men closed their mouths and followed their Major by flicking the safeties to off and resting their fingers on the trigger guards. Their movements were slower, more controlled as each man scanned the area.

“I miss me some gratuitous violence,” Muldoon said with a sigh.

Carter turned to the side. “What the fuck did the Major just fucking say?!” His face was bright red, and it looked like at any second the veins bulging on his neck would explode. Muldoon opened his mouth, but the second-in-command continued talking. “I swear to fucking god, you’re here just to fucking vex me. Right?”

The others shook as they fought the urge to burst into loud guffaws of laughter. Hearing this, Randolph Carter turned his bright red face to them and said, “What’s so fucking funny? You all heard Hank! Eyes open and mouths fucking shut, or I swear to god, I’ll sew them AND your assholes shut!”

He looked at Armitage and said the icing on the cake, “Sorry about that. I’ll make sure they stay quiet.”

CHAPTER THREE

The air was thick with the smell of death; that rotting rancid stench of shit, piss and decomposing flesh mixed, then left out in the blazing sun for days was like an old friend for The Cutthroats. With each step, the stench grew stronger and clung to their sinuses with steel claws.

"Well," Muldoon said as he snorted then spat, trying to get rid of the taste, "this is a lovely little vacation. When do we get to the topless bar and nudie beach?"

There was a collective groan from his teammates and the sniper chuckled, then stopped. His mouth dropped open and his hands trembled. The rattling of his gear caught the attention of Carter who sighed and said while turning, "Why am I not surprised it's you…"

His voice trailed off when he saw what had startled the soldier; large trees stained with blood, pox-marked by bullet holes and deep gashes made by blades. Dark red pools and puddles of blood covered the area. It was truly a view straight from hell, especially when the others started spotting the hunks of flesh and piles of bones littered about.

"Stop your gawking," Carter said. "We've all seen killing fields before. This isn't any different."

Gilman gagged, then coughed. He forced himself not to heave up his breakfast. That was the last thing he wanted to do in front of his brothers-in-arms. "Yeah," he said weakly. "But that isn't."

Following the man's trembling finger, the others saw a couple of spider-monkeys playing with a man's skull. They hooted in joy as they threw it back and forth, chasing each other around the bloody scene. The eye holes the perfect size and depth for their hooked hands to hold it. Both took no notice of the six shocked men nor the viscera and carnage they scampered through, their black fur now stained and matted by the blood.

Nightingale raised his M4A1, stared down the scope and aimed. "Give me the word," he rumbled while placing his finger on the trigger.

Carter turned to Armitage and was stunned to see a look of disgust on the man's face. "Hank?" the second-in-command asked with a gentle tap on the shoulder.

"The word is, 'No'," Armitage said then turned away. "Let's go," he said without another look at the surreal scene, "daylight's burning."

Slowly, each man turned and followed their leader until all that was left, watching the monkeys, was Nightingale and Carter. "That's just fucking wrong," the giant said. "Fucking wrong, I tell you."

"Preaching to the choir, mate," Carter said with a shake of his head. "Come on, big man," he said, tugging on the sleeve of the communications officer's shirt.

Sam Nightingale nodded and lowered his weapon. Feeling better, Carter turned and walked until he disappeared into the dense foliage. As Nightingale followed his friend, something heavy crashed into his back.

Spinning around, carbine rifle snapping up, the soldier saw floating in a puddle of crimson near his foot, a skull. Looking up, Nightingale spotted the two spider monkeys watching him intently. They smiled at him and hooted, trying to get him to throw back the skull and play with them.

Screwing the suppressor on to the end of the carbine's barrel, Nightingale aimed from the hip and squeezed the trigger gently.

A couple of pops filled the air and the spider monkeys fell to the ground; blood flowed from the large bullet holes that riddled the tiny bodies. One of the small furry bodies twitched and whimpered as the life left its body.

"Sam," Armitage's voice crackled through the man's earpiece, "where the fuck are you?"

"Coming, boss," the giant said as he quickly took off the suppressor and jogged away from the scene of carnage and death. He didn't bother to look back at his handiwork and if he had, Sam Nightingale would've seen something large, sleek and black swim through the blood and swallow the corpses in one mouthful.

It took the man only five minutes to catch up to the rest of the team, and the moment he crashed through the brush, The Cutthroats turned and applauded politely. Taken back by the reception, Nightingale smiled and bowed deeply. "Thank you, thank you, thank you," he said. "And for my next trick—"

"You'll learn to follow orders," Armitage said without a hint of amusement to his voice. "What the fuck were you doing? Having a shit?"

Nightingale opened his mouth, but the Major talked over him. "Doesn't matter. Don't fucking wander off without letting us know. We don't know what's out there, and none of us can afford to get lost. That helo is coming and if any of you miss it… I don't know when you'll be picked up. Got it?"

The giant nodded. He felt like he had just been chastised by his father and that was an impossibility since he never knew the man. "Sorry, Hank," Nightingale said, trying to sound like a professional. "Won't happen again."

With a nod, the Major turned and started walking again. "Let's keep it moving," he said. "We're already behind schedule."

Each man fell into place and Nightingale strode past them all. "I'll take point again," he said without asking.

Carter walked up next to his friend and fell into step easily. He didn't say a word. There was no need, since he knew that soon enough his comrade would start talking.

With each step, though, the silence continued and Randolph Carter felt awkward. "So," he said, taking the initiative, "that's one way to handle it… Want to tell me what the fuck that was?"

Armitage's eyes focused on the giant who moved easily

through the dense foliage. He had the rifle up and swept it back and forth in a wide arch. "This isn't like Siberia, or even Australia. We need to be even more careful than before."

"Why?" Ward asked, then immediately regretted speaking. His superiors turned as one and glared at the man, who slowed his pace and hid behind Gilman. "Are they still looking?" he asked meekly.

"Disney," Carter said, and relished the annoyed expression that flashed across the man's face, "keep young Charles here out of trouble. That's a good lad."

Gilman nodded, then slowed until Muldoon passed them. Happy with the result, Carter switched the channel until it was just him and Armitage on the line. "Answer the question."

"Switch it back," Armitage said. "They need to hear it too." He waited as static crackled until he heard Gilman and Ward speaking.

"Listen up," Carter said in his old drill Sargent voice. Immediately the men went silent, even though their boots continued crunching the dried leaves. "But don't go full retards. Eyes open."

Henry Armitage smiled. Even though they'd been together for many years and each knew what they had to do and how to behave, Carter still fell into the old ways of being a drill Sargent. The voice, mannerisms and expressions used got the men into action without a second thought. On the plus side, it amused Armitage to no end. "You done?" Armitage asked, and the rest of the men chuckled.

"Pipe down," the Major said, then cleared his throat. "We're in the middle of the Lacandon Jungle. For those who didn't read your intel-packet, this rainforest goes from Chiapas, Mexico all the way down to Honduras. The math wizards among us will tell you, that's approximately one point nine million hectares." He didn't pause to let the vastness work its way into the men. There was no time. "If you get lost in here, you're fucked."

"And not in the fun way," Muldoon added with a sad sigh. He waited for the laughter and jokes, but the eerie silence made him cough. "Sorry, boss."

Armitage waved his hand. "Apart from the jaguars, leeches,

scorpions, spiders AND poisonous frogs. The jungle holds something worse. Jorge Galindo, our target. We saw his handiwork back there," his eyes stared at Nightingale. "That was the remains of his enemies. The missing remains and body parts are all from the local wildlife. But, from what intel says, he's notoriously brutal with taking out rivals."

"Wait a minute," Ward said, interrupting the lesson. "This guy's our target? I thought we were picking up some package?"

"You need to listen better," Nightingale rumbled as he screwed the suppressor back onto the end of the rifle's barrel. He rolled his neck and shoulders, filling the air with a loud cracking.

"Doesn't matter," Armitage said, and his voice was hollow. "We need to get moving. There's no telling how many men or patrols he has out, especially this close to an execution zone." That point alone made his men look to Nightingale. The giant lowered his head in shame and the rifle slipped from his hand.

"No heroics," Carter said, trying his best to make his voice sound gentle and caring. "Heroes get killed, remember?"

"Yes, Sir," The Cutthroats answered as one.

Henry Armitage continued speaking. As he did, he walked faster and faster, "Sam, you have the right idea. I want suppressors on all weapons; the M4s and Kimbers. Headshots only. No loud noises. We're in full stealth mode for this one."

"Conserve your ammunition," Carter added, taking over for his Major. "Only take a shot if it's clear, and you know for a fact it'll kill them. No wounds, no chances. If you're not sure, double tap. Understand?"

Each of the men's eyes darted from one to the other. This was different to any other mission, and the secrecy of it all had them on edge.

"What else?" Nightingale asked, and the others nodded along. There were too many unanswered questions for their liking.

Armitage looked to the giant, "That's it." He sighed and seemed older than he was. "All the information they gave me is in the intel packs… No fucking way I'd leave you in the dark, but that's the situation. We're basically blind. Hence the over-precautions."

"Boss," Gilman said, and the anxiety in his voice made it

quiver slightly, "are we going to get fucked? Like Siberia?"

That was the question all the men wanted answered. The worst mission in the history of The Cutthroats. They hadn't fully recovered from it, nor had all the wounds healed. It was a fair question, and Armitage smiled slightly. "Not if I can help it," he said,

Muldoon spat then said, "Why does that Lee Marvin movie come to mind?" He looked at his brothers, "You know the one, right? It's got him, Trini Lopez, and—"

"The Dirty Dozen," Gilman said with a sigh. "Fuck, I hate that movie."

"Why?" Muldoon asked in mock surprise. "It's a great movie, ranks up there with The Great Escape and Inglourious Basterds and considering the circumstances, it's quite fitting."

"Nah," Ward said with a chuckle. "This is more in line with The Wild Geese."

"I'm Roger Moore, right?" Carter said, and that got a massive laugh from the men.

"Only if it's undead-ugly-as-sin Roger Moore," Armitage said with a shake of his head. The distraction provided by Muldoon was perfect, and he looked to the sniper.

Muldoon nodded, a slight gesture that said everything he needed to. "If that's the case, then Hank is Richard Burton," he said with a wolfish grin.

"Got a question," Nightingale said, and his voice ended the frivolity. "Why would he leave the bodies out like that? I mean, was it a warning for trespassers or something else?" He looked at Armitage, whose head was turned to the side. "Boss, you know these cartels are like cults and worship Death like a goddess?"

Carter scoffed then said, "When did you become a superstitious old woman?"

The giant didn't answer because Armitage spoke. "That's a good question. Let's go ask him," the Major said at the same time his team heard the voices that had distracted him.

CHAPTER FOUR

The branches and leaves smacked the men, leaving grazes and gashes as they quietly jogged through the thick jungle. Their movements were still precise, but with a swiftness that potential enemies brought.

"Hank," Carter whispered as the Team Leader crouched low and slipped through the large ferns and vines, "is this the best option? Can't we go around them?"

Armitage shook his head. "We can't leave any of them out here. Do you want to take on Galindo's men while having these guys behind us? I'm not holding aces and eights, you know," he said while screwing the suppressor to the front of his Kimber Gold handgun. His M4A1 was all good to go. The handgun was the last. "Are they ready?"

Carter blinked. Out of all the questions they could ask him, this was the one furthest down on the list. "Sir?" he asked without realising he'd forgotten the rules.

"Relax, mate," Armitage said with a small smile. He pressed the microphone and said, "We looking good?"

On either side of the men, in a line, the rest of The Cutthroats sounded their response by tapping on their mics three times. Looking to the left, then the right, Armitage saw the suppressor clad rifles and handguns. Whatever they were walking into, the six men would give it hell.

As they continued dropping to their knees and doing a waddle through the jungle, each man began their pre-combat ritual. Nightingale began, "Lo, there do I see my father. Lo, there do I see my mother."

"And my sisters, and my brothers. Lo, there do I see the line of my people," Muldoon said, his voice deep and solemn sounding.

"Back to the beginning," Ward finished the first part of the ritual and sighed in relief.

"Lo, they do call to me," Gilman started the second part in equal solemnity.

"They bid me take my place among them," Carter said as the men sensed the finale and the adrenaline pumping.

"In the halls of Valhalla!" Armitage said in a hushed roar.

"Where the brave may live forever!" The Cutthroats said in unison before slowing to a creeping movement. Each man sweated but did not feel the heat. The adrenaline flowing through their veins helped with that. Also, the Viking prayer always got them focused on the oncoming storm of violence. It centred them in a way nothing else did.

"I miss Stieg," Ward said with a sad sigh as the memory of the man who taught them the prayer came to his mind.

"Mourn him later," Armitage hissed as the voices grew louder.

A rough sounding voice, filled with hatred and an untouched rage said, "Aquí debería hacerlo. ¿Qué opina, jefe?"

"Esto es perfecto," a smooth, soft sounding voice replied. Even though it sounded gentle, there was a coldness to it. "Esperemos que esas malditas cosas no encuentren este lugar. ¿Qué carajo estás mirando?"

The first voice laughed. "Nunca antes había visto a un Dios de cerca," the man said as the sounds of crying and whimpering filled the air.

"No soy un Dios. Aunque está cerca," the second voice said with a chuckle that was bereft of humour. "Los quiero alineados, de rodillas. Lo haremos antes de que el almuerzo esté listo. Paula ha hecho cochinita."

"¡Ya lo has oído! ¡Ponte en la maldita fila ahora mismo!" the first voice bellowed. A second later, The Cutthroats heard the familiar sound of fists slamming into faces and men coughing up blood.

Carter looked to Armitage and raised an eyebrow. His finger flashed in the air. The simple sign language they had figured out to make stealth missions easier said, "That doesn't sound like a regular grunt. Do you think it's him?"

Armitage shook his head then peeked over the top of the bush he hid behind; the seven men, each looking like they had seven different levels of shit kicked out of them, rested on their knees with their heads down low. The blindfolds covering their bloodied eyes clung to the flesh. Each of the men sobbed as they came to the realisation that their day had finally come.

Standing before them were five armed men. One held a small phone up and recorded the scene. Next to him stood a man covered in scars and tattoos, his hateful eyes glared at the men and the malicious smile said it all. He owned the first voice.

On the other side of the cameraman stood Jorge Galindo. The light coloured skin made him look like a man with a tan, not a true Mexican. Hair slicked back and parted to the side gave him a distinguished businessman appearance. But there was an intensity to the way he stared at the kneeling, petrified men. His movements were as precise and measured as The Cutthroats' and he gave off the air of a caged animal.

Armitage turned to his men, letting his hands speak for him, "Nobody fucking moves until I give the signal. I want these fuckers completely focused. If we can take them out without alerting others, so much the better."

Each man gave a slight nod of the head and Ward's hands danced, "What about those on the ground?"

Carter shook his head, then pointed at the proceedings. All eyes went to the scene and Charles Dexter Ward's face contorted into a scowl.

"¿Ya estás grabando?" Galindo asked as Scarface walked up to the first man in line. He smiled as the metallic shriek of rusty metal grinding against metal cut through the air. The machete glinted in the sunlight, blinding the cameraman for a second, and

Scarface laughed.

The young man holding the camera nodded and said, "Sí, jefe." He trembled slightly and flinched at the gentle hand resting on his arm.

Galindo spoke softly, reassuringly, to the man, "Esto es un hecho de nuestra vida. Créeme, estos perros no pestañearían si estuvieras en su posición. Se reirían y luego buscarían a tu familia y le harían cosas indescriptibles a tus mujeres. ¿Es eso lo que quiere?" The way he spoke really reminded the crouched watching men of a politician. The drug-lord smiled at the young man then said, "Haz lo que tu conciencia diga."

Snot ran from the man's nose and he shook his head, "No. Soy un buen jefe. Terminemos con esto."

With a friendly pat, Galindo turned to his second and nodded. Scarface stared into the camera and said, "¡Este es un mensaje para todos los que intentan tomar lo que es nuestro!" The flat of the blade smacked the kneeling man's head hard enough to make him cry, "¡Diles quién eres, cabrón!"

A rough hand yanked back on the man's hair, revealing the face of a teen boy. Swollen flesh covered his right eye and half his nose was missing. "Me llamo Ernesto Islas. ¡Extraño a mi familia! Por favor, déjenme ir, señores," blood and mucus slightly muffled the voice. His good eye went to Galindo, and the man begged, "Mi esposa, señor, está embarazada. No quise robar—"

A dull wet thud filled the air and Ernesto's face went slack and lost the terrified expression. Dark red tendrils of blood ran down the gasping man's face, pooling in the open mouth until it overflowed and stained the jungle's floor.

With a wrenching movement, the machete's blade tore out of the cranium. Scarface grunted then giggled as fragments of skull and brain oozed up then dropped to the ground with splats. His bright evil eyes went to his boss, who didn't look away. It was like he was forcing himself to watch the carnage, and Galindo nodded.

"¡Nuestro mensaje será oído!" he barked before grabbing the dying man's hair. His muscles bulged from the effort as the slightly dulled blade bit into the skin with heavy smacks. Blood squirted from the impact, covering the men closest to the wound in crimson.

Each hit made the arms spasm and flail about. The sound of flesh being torn was horrendous, but the shriek of bone being scraped sent a shiver down the cameraman's spine.

The horrid sound of skin and muscle being sawed at and then the rip made the man almost throw up. Then he saw the severed head being held up for the camera and world to bask in. The camera shook, and the man wanted to flee, run back to his family and never set foot again in the Lacandon Jungle.

Galindo saw this and said, "Toma un respiro. Si quieres volver y tener una mujer, está bien. No hay que avergonzarse de dar la espalda."

"Pero, señor, ¿cómo no voy a mirar si usted se queda aquí sin pestañear, entonces yo también debería. Unidos estamos de pie," the man said with a reaffirming nod.

The drug-lord said nothing. He smiled and turned back to Scarface. "Sigue adelante;" he said with a wave of his hand.

The Cutthroats watched as the machete wielding maniac went down the line and decapitated the men. Four strikes to the side of the neck was all it took until there was a slight ripping sound mixed with a pop as each head came free. Scarface held up the head to the camera for a second before tossing it to the side and kicking the stiff body over.

"What do we do?" Ward's fingers frantically spoke for him. His face was pale and his body trembled. It was obvious he was breaking from the cruelty on display. "We have to do something!"

Armitage didn't see the medic. He was focused on Galindo's face; there was something about it that was strange. He'd seen warlords, drug-lords, killers of all natures stand before their handiwork and smile in delight. Galindo, on the other hand, looked like he was uncomfortable or remorseful with the violence being performed. *Why would you not enjoy this?* he thought before looking to his men.

He tapped his mic, then spoke. "Spread out," he said quickly. "We have one shot at this. Tommy, you and Disney take out Mister Machete. Randy and Charles stay here and keep an eye out," he looked to Nightingale and smiled. "Sam, you're with me. We're going after the package."

The Cutthroats tapped their mics and nodded. Carter scuttled over to Ward and placed a friendly hand on the young medic's arm. Immediately the man stopped shaking and nodded his thanks. They watched as Muldoon and Gilman moved to the other side of the clearing, keeping to the shadows.

Meanwhile, next to the stationary men, Nightingale and Armitage waited for the moment to rush in. They had their rifles cradled in their arms and had their OKC Spec Plus Bowie Knives out, ready to make quick work of any stragglers, or to cut Galindo's ankles.

"The word is yours," Armitage whispered into the comms and the four men waited.

"¿Por qué la prisa, jefe?" Scarface asked as he wiped the blade on a corpse's t-shirt. He hated to be rushed, especially when he was enjoying himself and killing was at the top of that list. He frowned in confusion and asked, "¿Estás bien?"

Jorge Galindo stared at the man, his head tilted slightly to the side in confusion. His mouth opened, and the man breathed, "Tienes algo en tu cara." He watched as the man reached up and wiped blood, skull and grey matter from his face. Scarface laughed at the perceived joke, then frowned when his boss said, "Todavía está ahí… En tu frente."

The tiny red dot wobbled as the man turned in place, trying to find whatever it was on his head. He grunted, wiping more of the viscera from his face. But the dot stayed right where it was. "¡¿Qué coño es esto, güey?!" he said while waving his arms wildly about his head.

There was a tiny pop, and Scarface flinched. His right eye rolled up and to the right as the optical nerve was severed.

A trail of blood ran down his face, following the contours of his face until it pooled in the corner of his mouth and entered his left eye. The man blinked, trying to rid his vision of the noxious liquid.

"¿Qué diablos está pasando?" Galindo said as another pop sounded and he felt the air next to his ear whoosh.

Scarface's head snapped back, and both eyes glazed over. His limbs went numb and limp, his nervous system severed by the second high-calibre bullet. Galindo watched in horror as his second-in-command collapsed straight down.

The man was dead. The remains of his brain oozing out of the twin bullet holes that had suddenly appeared in his head.

"¡Sáquenme de aquí!" the drug-lord said, spinning to the left and to his cameraman.

Another two pops filled his ears, and the young, terrified man coughed up blood as his throat exploded from the two bullets that ripped his voice-box to shreds.

With a gasp of shock, Galindo stepped back as blood sprayed his front. He felt his stomach churn and bile rise.

Holding his mouth, the man closed his eyes as another pop sounded. Opening his right eye slightly, the man saw the cameraman slump in the same way Scarface had.

Mind racing, the drug-lord spun, looking for the cunts who were attacking his boys. A single thought raced as he slipped on the piss and shit both bodies had deposited in their moment of expiration.

The most powerful drug-lord in Mexico fell flat on his ass with a loud thud and a comical sounding 'oof'.

He sighed and looked up at the smiling face of a giant wearing camouflage and military equipment.

"Hello there!" the giant rumbled before slamming a fist into the confused Galindo's face.

CHAPTER FIVE

The air whipped about, sending pieces of grass and chunks of bark into Galindo's face. The drug-lord winced, then opened his eyes. Bright, harsh, burning sunlight blinded him and he swiftly shut them again.

Around him he could hear men talking and laughing. The language was strange to his ears, most likely English, and his mind started working.

"Fuck me, he doesn't look like a butcher," Muldoon said, staring intently at the bound and gagged man. "More like an accountant or engineer to me."

Nightingale shook his head. "They never do," he said while holding a radio microphone to his mouth. "Please repeat," he said, trying to sound as calm as possible. "Last message was garbled as fuck! Please repeat!"

He looked at Armitage and Carter with an apologetic shrug. "These flyboys are all the same."

The Cutthroats laughed as one unit. Each man had their own interesting tale when dealing with other parts of the military. Especially when it came to other countries'.

"Not as bad as the Brits," Ward said, "remember that shit storm we were dropped in over in China? The Wu-Han job."

"Don't fucking remind me," Gilman said, rolling his eyes while scratching his right knee. "This still hurts when it's cold," his hand pointed to it and again he scratched an imaginary itch. "Fucking government spooks."

Again the men laugh and Galindo slowly opened his eyes again, letting them acclimate to the sunlight breaking through the jungle's canopy. The wind continued to blow and the rapid movement of the trees blowing didn't help. Once his eyes had adjusted enough, they darted to the faces of each man. Luckily for Jorge Galindo, he had a mind for faces and could pick any man out of a line-up years after a meeting.

It was obvious these men were military, not cartel, which had its own set of pros and cons. The biggest one being he was still alive. That reason only told him everything he needed to know, and it made him smile.

"Awwww, look at 'im," Muldoon said, mimicking the voice of a proud parent. "Trying to smile… they grow up so fast," he said, looking at the others. "Makes you proud, doesn't it?"

"Shut up," Armitage said. He was sitting on a fallen log and had both eyes on the tied-up drug-lord. "Keep your eyes on the package," he spoke sharply and Galindo knew this man was the leader. "Until the EVAC is here, we're on high-alert."

As Muldoon sighed and stretched languidly, the team's medic kneeled down next to the decapitated bodies and inspected each of them while shaking his head. "This was messy as fuck," Ward said in disgust. "You'd think these 'hardened killers' would know how to do the job with no problems."

"Fucking amateurs," Gilman said to Carter, who was checking his copy of the map. The second-in-command frowned as his eyes followed the trail marked in red sharpie. "What is it?"

Carter shook his head, "It must've been dumb-fucking luck we stumbled upon him when we did." The man looked up at the TL and he whispered, "We're about fifteen klicks from his supposed compound. It doesn't make any sense why he'd be out here."

Armitage shrugged; he didn't believe in coincidences or luck, but this was one of the few moments he had to agree with his friend, "Dumb fucking luck indeed."

The radio crackled with static, then a Texan sounding voice said, "Come in CT-666. Repeat, come in CT-666. This is Raptor 1128 inbound. We're about five minutes away. Are you in position? Repeat, are you in position?"

The Cutthroats cheered, except for Armitage. He crouched low, eyes staring at the prisoner and pondering how come a drug-lord like Jorge Galindo would be out in the field doing the dirty work. It didn't matter though; he didn't speak any Spanish, and the dossier mentioned nothing about the man knowing English. What did matter was the mission was a success with minimal casualties.

"Hear that?" Nightingale boomed with a massive smile. Using his boot, the giant nudged the ex-drug-lord and said, "Soon you'll be getting fucked seven ways from Sunday!"

Muldoon chuckled before muttering, "That's a lot of Sundays."

"You're telling me," Ward said in a shocked tone. "Wonder how an asshole would look after that?"

Nightingale smiled maliciously, "Whoever said he'd be getting fucked there?" he said with a low laugh. The communications officer had a nasty streak that only came out when dealing with a real nasty.

"What do you have against our guest?" Muldoon asked. His eyes focused on the Major and there was something about his concerned, irritated expression that worried the man.

Charles Dexter Ward spoke for the giant. "Isn't it obvious why? Our guest here has caused countless deaths, disappearances and god-only knows what else. Not to mention the thousands of lives ruined or snuffed out because of his drugs flowing without restrictions."

As the Team's medic continued his sermon, Armitage watched the bound man's face. Instead of anger, which is what he expected, Galindo wore a look of regret and remorse and that surprised Armitage. The more Ward spoke, listing the crimes, the horrors and atrocities perpetrated by the man on the jungle's floor, the more Galindo appeared to be human. Even Armitage, a man who had been through hell and back, seen the worse of humanity, couldn't believe what Ward was saying. Most of the acts were not in the profile. "That's enough," he said, ending the oral attack.

Ward looked to his commander in surprise. "What is it, boss?" he asked as the rest of the team looked up at the sky. The trees rocked and swayed as the roar of an approaching helicopter drowned out the sounds of the jungle.

"Eyes open," Carter said as he nodded at Muldoon and Gilman, then pointed to Galindo. "I want him bagged and ready to go the moment the helo lands."

"What about me?" Ward asked as the two men pulled a black velvet sack over the criminal's head, then yanked him to his feet.

Armitage stood and stretched, "You and Sam will keep your eyes open. Anything strange, yell out. Anyone who shouldn't be here, put them down." He looked to the giant, then back to the medic, "Clean headshots only. Okay? Do not waste your ammo."

The two nodded before looking to the perimeter of the small clearing they were in.

"What's up?" Carter asked as he readied his weapon for transportation.

"Call it a feel—" Armitage's voice turned into a grunt of pain as his head snapped back and dark crimson exploded from his face.

"Hank!" Randolph Carter shouted as he dropped to the ground, while Jorge Galindo used his shoulder to shove his captors to the side.

The voices rang out as the loud gunfire from AK-47s shattered the jungle's tranquility. "¡Tienen al jefe!" one bellowed as high above the men, another UH-60 Black Hawk helicopter came into view.

"¡Maten a estos malditos!" another voice shouted as The Cutthroats ducked to the ground.

"What the fuck is going on?" Muldoon said as his eyes watched the helo. "How's the TL?"

Carter raised his M4A1 and squeezed the trigger. In the distance he heard a scream of pain followed by, "¡Hijo de puta!" The man smiled as his free hand rolled Armitage over; blood ran from the mess that had once been his right eye. He was pale, but his chest rose and fell.

"Captain?" Gilman said, staring through the scope of his rifle. He had his elbow jammed into Galindo's ribs, keeping the man down and in pain.

Next to them, Nightingale held the radio to his mouth and screamed, "Raptor, do not land! Repeat, do not land! We are under fire. We are under fucking fire!"

"Count them off," Carter said as he patted his friend's shoulder. Armitage groaned and his left eye fluttered open. "Don't take potshots. If you get a clean shot, you fucking take it!"

Ward crawled across the ground, his fatigues getting dirtier as he dragged himself through the mud and leaves. "How's the wound?" he asked the moment he got to Carter and Armitage.

"He'll live," the Captain said as bullets whizzed over their heads and punctured the trees behind them. "Get him patched up and ready to go." He didn't bother waiting for the medic to speak, "Listen up killers, that helo won't wait around much longer. So, here's the plan—"

"Gratuitous violence all the way!" Muldoon crowed as he took aim and fired in the space of a second. There was a groan followed by the thud of leaves being crushed and the gunfire stopped.

In the silence, the soldiers could hear one of their attackers say, "¿Cómo diablos hizo eso?"

"¡No es justo!" another said while The Cutthroats used their scopes to locate their attackers. Hiding behind fallen branches, hanging vines, and tree trunks were seven sicarios that all had one thought running through their brains; do not let the gringos take Galindo. If that happened, their lives were well and truly fucked.

"¡No importa!" a gruff voice that was obviously the men's leader bellowed. "¡Maten a estos malditos!"

Carter shook his head. These guys were definitely amateurs in sore need of a lesson. "Sam," he said into his comms, "how many you got?"

"Seven little Indians," the giant said with a laugh.

Gilman and Muldoon both nodded and held up a thumb, signalling they had the same count. Above their heads the bullets continued to speed through the air, the sound of wood being punctured and animals crying out in pain showed just how ineffective the Narcos were.

"On the count of three," Carter said as he readied himself, "take as many of them out as possible." His eyes caught Galindo, who was shaking his head and mumbling, trying to speak around the ball-gag and bag. “Moment they’re down, Sam, call in the helo.”

The three other men tapped their mics two times, and Carter felt his muscles tense from the expected fight. “One,” he said. “Two. Fire”

At once, Gilman, Muldoon and Nightingale rose to a kneeling position and fired, their fingers squeezing the triggers in short, controlled motions. Each M4A1 carbine rifle popped, the suppressors doing their jobs, and the ejected bullet shells clanged to the ground.

Mists of blood mixed with grey matter sprayed into the air as the bullets tore through the Narcos’ foreheads. Each man screamed and flailed above, the AK-47s still firing as the fingers clamped down, muscles tensing from the damaged nervous system.

“Cease fire,” Armitage’s voice was weak but still commanding. “Confirm the kills,” his left eye glared at Ward then went to Carter. “What the fuck happened?”

“A shit-storm, for lack of a better term,” Carter said by way of explanation. “You’re going to need an eye-patch.”

“Though you’ll be quite the badass,” Ward said as they heard Nightingale stomping through the jungle. His heavy footsteps crunched the dry leaves and snapped twigs and gave the impression he was a giant. “Give Snake Plissken a run for his money anyway,” the medic said as he finished wrapping a heavy-duty gauze around the Major’s head.

As the two men helped Armitage to his feet, the sound of a Kimber Gold handgun being fired in succession could be heard. After each shot they heard the communications officer roll a body then mutter, “Another one bites the dust.”

“How’s the package?” Armitage asked as the giant returned to the clearing and pulled out his radio.

Gilman and Muldoon hauled the bagged Galindo to his feet and roughly patted him down. The man winced from the roughness. “He’s fine. Just a little dirty is all,” Gilman said.

“Boss,” Ward’s voice was filled with concern, “you shouldn’t be moving around too much. There’s no way to know what internal injuries you’ve sustained.”

Armitage waved the medic away as he nodded to Nightingale. "Get them down."

"Raptor, this is CT-666, you are cleared for landing," the giant said into the radio. The men looked up as the Black Hawk began its descent towards the clearing.

"¡Jefe! ¡Corre!" a weak voice shouted.

The Cutthroats turned in time to see a Narco raise a PSRL-1 RPG into the air and fire. Shielding themselves from the bright harsh light from the ignition, the missile hit the helicopter.

A second later, the weapon exploded. Shards of the projectile pierced the haul of the aircraft, severing control lines and the fuel tank. An errant spark happened and the fuel tank erupted.

The Cutthroats stared in disbelief as the Black Hawk exploded and the fiery remains crashed to the ground, sending the men diving out of the way.

CHAPTER SIX

"What the flying fuck was that?!" Armitage demanded as his nostrils filled with the pungent odour of burning gasoline. He turned to Nightingale, "I thought you tagged them all!"

The Major's face was red, veins throbbed in his neck and the bloody stain on the bandage grew larger and darker. As he paced back and forth, Carter and Nightingale busied themselves with trying to put out the burning wreckage. They scooped up handfuls of damp earth and flung it into the flames.

Meanwhile, Gilman and Muldoon had their Kimbers pointed at Galindo's head. The drug-lord was on his knees with the bag hanging from his neck. His eyes focused on the dead bodies of his men, who were neatly piled together.

"Answer me!" Armitage bellowed at Nightingale. "You had one fucking job!"

Carter stood with a groan, turned to the Major and said, "Hal, you need to calm the fuck down." He stared at the one-eyed man who looked fit to be tied and didn't stop. "It doesn't matter what happened or who's to blame. What DOES, is that we finish the fucking mission. Right?"

The two men locked eyes in a deadly silence. The only sound that could be heard was the crackling of the fire and the heavy breathing of the men. Not a soul dared to speak. The Cutthroats knew better than to get between a fight between the Major and the Captain, while Galindo couldn't because the ball-gag was still blocking his mouth and now he felt his jaw aching and drool running down his front.

"Right?" Carter said again and his tone said it all: don't fucking say anything else. It was a well-known tone of voice. In fact, it was part of what had drawn Armitage to recruiting Carter in the first place. He was a Drill Instructor and could turn any and all into sniveling children wanting their mummies and daddies. "Right?" he asked for a third time, and the tone came out even more forcefully.

The single eye darted to the scorched jungle floor and focused on the pools of blood that were already almost dried. He knew Carter had a point; he was acting like a spoiled child. But there was nothing more important than the mission and his men. That was what set him off. The fact that if they were already in the helicopter and airborne, they'd all be dead.

"Siberia won't happen again," Armitage said softly, and his voice caught everyone off guard.

Nightingale blinked then lowered his head saying, "Sorry, boss. Won't let it happen again. Promise." He continued to throw clumps of dirt onto the flames, but it was useless.

Galindo struggled against his restraints and started speaking. Unfortunately, his gag made it impossible for his captors to understand him. The two men with the guns pointed at him looked at each other, then one said, "Boss, looks like we've got a chatty-Cathy here."

Armitage looked over at the drug-lord and there was something in the man's eyes that spoke to him. But there was no time to indulge their prisoner. "Leave him be," he said, turning back to Carter.

The Captain hadn't moved or stopped staring at him and truth be told it was intimidating as hell.

"Sammy," Armitage said with an apologetic shrug, "you're one of the best… I didn't mean to leap down your throat." The Major grunted then rubbed his eye. "This fucking thing itches so much."

"You done having your domestic in public?" Carter said, using his eyes to gesture towards Galindo. "So much for being 'professionals'," he added with a shake of his head. "Think I'll look for another squad. One with true men of honour."

"Yeah, yeah, yeah," Armitage said, waving away the empty threat. "You've made your point. Tell me how it feels when you lose an eye AND miss a pickup."

"The firefight was fun," Muldoon said, cutting the tension easily, "real fun. But my favourite part was when the helo exploded." He looked at his brothers-in-arms and smiled weakly. "It was like something out of a Michael Bay movie! Imagine how it would've looked in slow motion!" He shuddered from the mental image.

Armitage and Carter exchanged weirded-out looks as Ward shifted uncomfortably. "Did he just cum?" Carter asked incredulously.

"I don't want to know," Armitage replied with a shudder of disgust. "You're a sick puppy," he said to Muldoon before looking at Nightingale. "Sammy, stop that, it's pointless," he walked over to the giant. "Get on the horn. I want another helo inbound ASAP."

"Not here," Nightingale rumbled, the unasked question explicit as the two men looked at the flaming wreckage; it was beyond repair, and the still strapped in bodies of the pilots continued to sizzle. The charred, blackened skin had the same appearance and texture of burnt bacon. Pieces of flesh peeled back, revealing dark bones, and the mouths were nothing more than a grim semblance of a smile. It was eerie, and the giant shook the feeling from his shoulders.

"Get me the tags," Armitage said as his eye watched the fire dance and consume the aircraft and the passengers. "Randy, think there's anything salvageable?"

The Captain didn't think or say a word. He stalked over to the downed helicopter and his eyes darted about, taking in everything. "Possible," he said before turning to Gilman. "Disney, give me a hand, okay? Ward, take his place guarding the package."

At the word 'package', Galindo renewed his struggles. His mouth moved in tight movements and his voice sounded like a rabid dog's snarl. Muldoon, Gilman, and Ward stepped back from the man and stared as the drug-lord fought to get to his feet.

"Get him under control!" Carter shouted as he drew his own handgun.

Galindo took the soldiers' momentary inaction to run towards the one-eyed Major. He panted and stumbled while still trying to talk around the ball-gag, saliva continued to dribble from his mouth and it covered his button-down shirt, making it cling to his chest.

A gloved fist slammed into his gut and the Mexican doubled-over before sinking to his knees. His head snapped back as the hand gripped his short hair and the barrel of the handgun was shoved into his left eye.

"You ever seen what happens to a head when it's shot at point blank range?" Carter said in a deathly quiet voice. "It's a thing of beauty, the way the bullet pierces the eyeball, rupturing the protective sack that holds the juices and iris. Then the moment of nothing as it rips and tears through the skull, shattering the bone and digging a tunnel into the brain."

Galindo's eyes went wide for a second and the Captain pressed his advantage. "The thing that makes this a piece of art is when the bullet exits the back of the head. With the right calibre of bullet, the entire cranium explodes and everything is sent flying in all directions. Ignore the movies," he smiled as he spoke, "reality is not clean or PG, in fact the human brain has a very distinctive smell."

Nightingale looked to Armitage and said, "Does it really smell?"

Both their eyes went to Ward, who was trying his best to hide the smile and laughter. He turned away and Armitage knew Carter was bullshitting like there was no tomorrow.

"Now," the Captain said while still smiling pleasantly, his voice was more conversational now which added to the disturbing nature of his speech, "if you don't want to become part of this ongoing art exhibit, might I suggest you don't fucking move or speak without explicit permission. Sound good?"

"He doesn't understand English..." Muldoon said, but his voice trailed off when the drug-lord nodded his head slowly.

"Ta," Carter said while stuffing the Kimber back into its holster. He nodded at Ward and Muldoon, who ran over and hooked their arms under his shoulders.

As they led the forlorn man away from Armitage, Carter used his index finger to beckon for Gilman. "Come on, Daisy," he said. "Little man with a big job."

"I'm taller than you!" Gilman said as he trudged over to the wreckage.

Carter continued to smile as he said, "Not what I was referring to."

It took a second for the joke to land, but when it did, The Cutthroats erupted into roars of laughter. That was the power of Randolph Carter. He got everyone moving when they had to or he could be the most intimidating mother-fucker on the planet and there was nobody else Armitage wanted by his side in a fight.

"Nicely done, Rosie," Armitage said, patting the Captain on the shoulder. Before the other man could answer, he turned to Nightingale and said, "Let's call a taxi."

"I'd rather an Uber," Muldoon shouted as the two men walked away from the wreck. He looked to Ward and said, "Last time I got in one, the young lady driver and I had a detour… If you know what I mean?"

Ward didn't blink as he said, "How much extra did she charge… Waitaminute!" He turned to his friend and his eyes sparkled. "Was that the one who turned out to be a tranny?"

"What? No! Shut the fuck up," Tommy Muldoon said as his face was flushed red. His eyes went to Galindo, who was trying to laugh himself. "Remember how the Captain explained what will happen to your head if he shoots? Well, my gun will be jammed so far up your arse, you'll think you're a spit-roast."

"What the fuck does that even mean?" Armitage said as he tapped his earpiece. "You really need help, Tommy," he said with a small chuckle as the communications officer pulled out the radio and dialled in the frequency.

"HQ, this is CT-666. Please respond," Nightingale said before depressing the talk button. He looked down at Armitage, "Do you think they'll respond?"

Henry Armitage didn't look back or reply immediately, his

eye focused on their prisoner. There was something about the way he moved, spoke and acted that made little sense, but then again the entire operation didn't add up. He made a mental reminder to speak with Carpenter when they got back to base-camp. "Try again," he said as he looked at Carter and Gilman.

The two men were busy tossing more dirt onto the flames, then stomping on it until plumes of smoke billowed from under the smothered fire. They moved methodically, but were avoiding the cockpit which was smart.

"Come in, HQ. This is CT-666. Come in HQ—"

"CT-666 this is HQ. Over. Status report," the gruff voice on the other end of the radio sounded annoyed with having to do actual work.

Armitage grabbed the radio and spoke quickly. "First things first, solider. Switch this channel over to a secure line of communication. Second, this is Major Armitage. Get me someone with power and if you can't find anyone, get Carpenter," he said with a grin. It was always fun to swing his dick around and get shit done quickly.

"Sir! Yessir!" the officer's voice crackled and the telltale sound of static hissing came from the speaker.

"Having fun?" Carter asked as he and Ward pulled the final salvageable ammunitions crate from the twisted hull. They had amassed five crates and were now eyeballing the cockpit. The flames were lower, but the sizzling sound coming from the carcasses told them otherwise.

Armitage nodded then turned back to Nightingale, saying, "Get me those tags. Or at least give me the names of the fly-boys."

"Report, Hank," Carpenter's voice sounded distant through the tiny radio's speaker and even older. "Shouldn't you be airborne by now?"

"Sitrep is FUBAR, Sir," Armitage said, trying to sound confident. "The helo is out of action, but the package is secured—"

"What the fuck happened, Major?"

"Sir," Armitage said as he ignored the disappointed tone in the General's voice, "the package's men ambushed us. A skirmish ensued, but the helo was caught by a missile." He caught the mangled dog-tags Carter tossed to him and read the names, "We lost Browne and Perez, though."

"What's your position?"

"At rally point alpha," Armitage said as a deep rumbling sound filled his ears; it was a rhythmic thudding that reminded him of artillery firing. Looking around, he saw the rest staring at the surrounding jungle. The sound grew louder as it closed in on the seven men. "Sir, request another EVAC at a different rally point. This one is compromised."

He didn't hear what Carpenter said, instead he focused on the thudding that now sounded like heavy footsteps mixed with trees creaking and snapping. Armitage didn't know what was approaching, but whatever it was, it was big.

"Major!" Carpenter's voice cut through the air like a whip. "Confirm that rally point delta will be used."

"Rally point delta," Armitage repeated. "We'll be there."

"Boss," Muldoon said, finishing the conversation with General Carpenter, "what would be the last thing you'd expect to see in the middle of the Mexican jungle?" There was something in his voice none of the others had ever heard: disbelief and astonishment.

Carter spun towards the man, "This is not the time…" his voice failed him as he saw what had caught the sniper's attention. "Fuck me!"

The radio went dead as Henry Armitage, leader of The Cutthroats, let the device slip from his hand. His mind couldn't believe what it was hearing; chirping and clicking that reminded him of animals communicating. "What the fuck is that?"

CHAPTER SEVEN

Behind the wreckage, standing over four metres tall, was an ant. The massive segmented body trembled slightly as the man-sized antennae swiveled and moved about, tracking the sounds and movements of the tiny men. Pitch black segmented eyes stared unblinkingly at the seven men and the serrated mandibles clicked and clacked.

"That's an ant," Sam Nightingale said the moment his brain started working. None of the gathered men could believe what they were seeing, least of all him. But there it was, an actual giant ant.

Muldoon giggled uncontrollably then said, "It's like 'Honey I Shrunk the Kids'."

"Shut the fuck up!" Carter snapped, turning to the man. "For once in your goddamn life, shut the fuck up. Please!"

The moment the Captain shouted, the ant flinched and moved towards the men. Its spiked feet pierced the ground with heavy steps that shook the trees. It ignored the flames and used a limb to demolish the smoking corpse of the helo into the ground. Nothing would stop it from eating.

Armitage shut his eye and shook his head. Maybe he had a concussion from the wound? Opening his eye and seeing the ant still approaching them, the realisation that there was more to the world than he knew slammed into his gut and he chuckled.

"What's so funny?" Carter said as he snapped the slide back on his M4A1 before bringing it up to his shoulder. "You found another movie reference perfect for this?"

The Major shook his head as his tactical mind and training took over. No matter what happened, he couldn't allow Galindo nor his men to be killed… or worse. "Tommy, you and Ward stay right where you are. Keep our guest company," he said while readying his own rifle for the fight. "Disney, you and Randy take the legs out. Sammy—"

He rolled at the same moment one of the long, hardened legs crashed down where he had been.

Coming up into a kneel, the soldier squeezed the trigger. He felt the carbine kick from the force of the exiting bullets and when it threw off his aim, Armitage released the trigger.

The ant squealed as it recoiled from the attack. The tiny pieces of lead bit into its exoskeleton and the pain was different to anything it had ever experienced. Spinning around to face the man, its abdomen collided with the tail of the helicopter, launching it into the air.

"Move your ass!" Nightingale bellowed to Muldoon as his eyes followed the path of the heavy, still burning metal.

Turning without a second to lose, Tommy Muldoon and Charles Dexter Ward pulled the wide-eyed drug-lord out of the way. With a tremendous crash that sent more flames and dirt high into the air, the hunk of metal landed.

"Fucking kill this thing!" Armitage snarled as he fired again. It felt strangely good to cause any amount of damage to the monstrous insect, even if it was minuscule.

Out of the corner of his eye he saw Nightingale crouch low to the ground and squeeze the trigger.

A wail of agony filled the air as the ant's left eye was riddled with tiny holes. Bright green liquid exploded from the wounds and the bug thrashed about, trying with all its might to dislodge whatever was eating its eye. The green continued to dribble and ooze from the wounds and red joined it, mixing to become a horrendous colour of pain.

"If it bleeds," Carter said as he and Gilman fired at the legs, "we can kill it!"

Muldoon whooped in ecstasy. "Now who's quoting movies!" he said as the Captain and Spotter tried to take out the giant legs; each shot, even though carefully placed, seemed to do nothing to slow the ant's maneuverability. It continued to stab at the closest man, which was Armitage.

"Boss!" Ward said in a panicked voice. "Shouldn't you get back?"

His carbine continued to fire in short controlled bursts, but it was obvious to Armitage that they'd need something bigger to take out the creature. "New plan," he said, rolling out of the way of another piercing jab. "Sam and I'll keep it distracted—"

"What?" the giant's voice cracked ever-so, and the men laughed despite the danger before them. "You want me to what?"

"Long as we keep moving and firing," Armitage said as he struggled to breathe, "it'll buy them enough time to find some heavy ordinance. Right?"

"Kaboom!" Muldoon said with a child-like laugh that landed him a death-glare from Carter. "Sorry," he said, hiding his enjoyment; out of all The Cutthroats, Tommy Muldoon was the craziest, with a lust for life that bordered on the deranged. "Tap me in, Coach!" he shouted, trying to get Armitage's attention.

"Permission to put one in his face?" Nightingale asked with a groan as he continued to fire his rifle in short controlled bursts.

Carter zig-zagged through the ant's legs with ease. "Get in line," he said as he spun and shot up into the belly of the insect. The bullets tore through the first layer of hard shell but did not physically damage it. Rolling from under, avoiding the tilted head and snapping mandibles, the man said, "Worth a try!"

"No heroics!" Armitage barked as he aimed for the segment gap between the front and back of the insect. He knew it wouldn't do any damage, but he had to keep it from going after his friend and the medic.

His aim was true, and the three short bursts of fire found their new home.

A jet of dark red blood spurted from the hits and the ant dropped to the right, antenna swivelling in confusion as its legs spasmed. A high-pitched whine came from its mouth and the seven men heard angry chittering answer the call for help.

"Think it just called for its mates," Carter said as he and Ward tore into the ammo crates. Each time they broke the seal and opened, the men were greeted with the pristine sight of fully loaded clips and grenades. But no missiles or high calibre rounds. "No fucking luck," the Captain swore as he and the team's medic loaded their packs with fresh clips and grenades.

Armitage didn't hear him. He was too busy focusing on the rapid flow of blood coming from the segment gap. "Sammy," he said as the ant continued to whine and fumble to stand, "think we can do something to help it?"

The communications officer was already ahead of him and had pulled out a frag grenade. He hefted it twice as the chittering from the reinforcements grew louder and the men felt the earth shake and the trees sway even more.

Silently, the giant took two steps, pulled the pin and threw it at the struggling ant.

There was a metallic clink as the explosive device bounced off the exoskeleton and landed with a dull thud under the monster.

"You've got to be fucking kidding me," Armitage said, looking at Nightingale who shrugged innocently. "Remind me not to play cricket with you."

"That's just mean," Nightingale said as he lifted his weapon, peered into the scope and flicked the rifle from automatic to single-shot mode. A bead of sweat rolled down his nose and pooled in the corner of his eye. With a grunt, he quickly fired one shot before using his sleeve to clear away the liquid.

Another tiny eruption of blood happened, and the bug collapsed on top of the expectant grenade. It rolled to the side and the tiny oval-shaped device penetrated the open wound with a wet squish. The legs thrashed and flailed about wildly as the ant cried out in fear and panic, the sound reminiscent of a dog's scared whimper mixed with a bird's frantic chirping.

The men heard a tiny pop and a second later the ant exploded in a grisly fountain of blood, guts, muscle and hunks of black hard shell. Each of the six legs flew into the air, hovered for a second, then came tumbling back to earth.

"Don't fucking move!" Armitage shouted as he tracked the

trajectory of the high-velocity stakes. "Wait until the last minute then scram."

One leg crashed into the gigantic corpse's head, impaling the brain and causing the eye to erupt from the pressure.

Muldoon smiled and laughed. He lived for the carnage, then he gasped. Without warning, he shoved Galindo into Ward and the two men fell to the blood-covered ground as the sniper dove. Another of the stakes slid into the ground right where he had just been standing. "Fuck yeah," he shouted as the remaining four legs returned to the earth's surface.

Each impact sent a tremor through the ground that shook the men and threw blood, body parts and branches into the air. The trained soldiers easily dodged the legs, and when the final one imploded against a tree trunk, they all looked at the fiery remains of the ant.

"Fuck me, that was more fun than Bali!" Muldoon said with a whoop. His hands ran over his body and he sighed in relief: no injuries.

Carter shook his head, then turned. A low growl filled the clearing that was mixed with clicks. "Give us five-fucking minutes!" he shouted at the three other gigantic ants waiting at the tree-line.

Each stared at the bloody scene and the antennae were all pointed at the still burning body of their brother. The mandibles opened and shut slowly, as if they were talking and the massive bodies trembled with uncontrollable rage.

"Tommy," Armitage said while rolling his shoulders, "make them re-think whatever they are thinking. Okay?"

The sniper was already ahead of his commanding officer; his hands were finishing piecing together his Heckler & Koch HK417 rifle and the moment the barrel clicked in place, the man smiled and caressed it lovingly. "Sheila's happy to speak with the interlopers," he said as he brought his eye to the scope and lay on the wet earth.

Gilman looked at the prone man, then to Carter, "Why did he go with Sheila?"

"Ask him yourself," the Captain said as he rolled two grenades between his hands. He didn't like the situation at all, but there was nothing to be done about it. "Let the man work, though."

The five special operations officers and Galindo watched as with all the skill of a master, Tommy Muldoon found the perfect target, pulled back the bolt of the rifle, took a deep breath, then exhaled slowly while he squeezed the trigger.

Jorge Galindo flinched from the crack of the round fired, and the man felt a trickle of piss fill his underwear.

The closest ant's head snapped to the left, and the body rocked. It turned towards the source of the sound and its pain; the eye was completely gone, now it resembled a broken mirror with shards of the segments hanging loosely. Blood flowed from the wound, and the muscles and nerves inside twitched and throbbed with instinctual movements.

It chirped and the three, four-meter tall monsters charged into the clearing.

Another loud cracked sounded and the bullet tore through the lead insect's head. The bullet shredded the muscle, bore into the brain cavity and in a glorious eruption, exited the back of the ant's skull. A jet of blood and grey matter covered its neighbour, while another two rounds ended the life of another ant.

"Nice shooting, Tex!" Nightingale said with a big smile that instantly faded. "On your six," he said, signalling to both Muldoon and Ward to spin.

Another four ants crashed through the trees and charged the three men. Galindo shook his arms, trying to get them free of his bonds, but the two soldiers were busy. Ward had a hand on the drug-lord's chest and was pushing him back as Muldoon used the HK417 to keep the new attackers at bay.

On the other side of the clearing, the third ant charged Carter and Gilman. The Captain didn't hesitate at all, his thumbs pulled the pins and he threw the grenades with ease.

The double explosion eviscerated the ant's head in a ball of fire, blood and exoskeleton. The body shook, then collapsed on top of the mangled rotor blades of the helicopter. Gilman stared at his friend in awe and the Captain said, "No time for love, Doctor Jones."

"We need to move out!" Armitage shouted as his M4A1 roared with each squeeze of the trigger. "Ward, cut Galindo free!

We're going for a run."

CHAPTER EIGHT

The men barrelled and crashed through the jungle with only one thought racing through their heads: *get away from the fucking ants!*

Nothing else mattered as each of the seven men could hear the trees groaning, bending then snapping behind them. The ants' size and bulk made quick work of the foliage; they moved as one mass; legs, mandibles and antennae came together to form a wall of terror that pushed the fleeing men further and further into the jungle.

"How much longer are they going to be playing chasies with us?" Muldoon grunted as he fought to breathe.

Armitage didn't know, which made the Major uneasy. Quickly he looked down at the map and his eye traced the path they were taking. "There should be a ravine up ahead. We get there and cause them to stampede right off the side."

"Tremors all the way," Nightingale rumbled, then looked at Carter and Gilman next to him. "What? I watch movies too."

"Well kaloo-kalay," the Captain said as he ducked under a branch, "maybe you can use that knowledge on the fucking gigantic ants behind us!"

A soft accented voice startled the men, "I don't think the

bichos would care."

Carter spun, continuing to backpedal as he stared in disbelief at Jorge Galindo. The man was pumping his arms and legs, keeping pace with the trained soldiers, and somehow he had removed his ball-gag. "What was that?" the soldier asked.

"The hormigas, I doubt they would understand your references… or your idioma," the drug-lord said as he leapt over a log with ease. His feet touched the ground, and he continued at the same pace. The only sign of exertion was the puffing from his mouth and the tiny beads of sweat dribbling from his face.

Armitage shook his head. *Of fucking course the man could speak English*, he thought. Whoever was in charge of the intelligence needed a good talking too, if they got out of this. "The ravine," he said to the man, "will it work?"

"No sé," Galindo said seconds before he stumbled and fell face first into a puddle of mud. His arms flailed about as he fought to get up and breathe.

Carter saw the man and laughed, then his training kicked in. "Ward! Get him up and moving!"

The medic grunted as he hastily pulled the man to his feet. "Off you go," he said with a firm shove in the right direction that sent Galindo stumbling. He turned back and glared at the soldier, then his eyes went wide and he bolted.

Ward turned and in one smooth motion he threw a grenade right at the gaping maw of an ant.

The tiny explosive device entered with no trouble, the ant stopping from the strange sensation in its mouth. The other ants followed suit and slowed until they gathered around their brother. Their chirps and clicks of curiosity sounded like a cartoon, but the razor-sharp mandibles clacking proved otherwise.

"Have a rest, boys," Carter said as he smiled patiently. Luckily, he didn't have to wait for long.

A flash of light blinded the men and as the momentary blindness faded, a thunderous explosion engulfed the area. The ant's head cracked, then erupted from the force of the grenade's design. The right antenna ripped through the eye of another ant while the flames vaporised the left one. The mandibles spun outwards like buzz-saw blades and sliced the bottom half of another ant's face off.

Blood and shards of exoskeleton flew, covering The Cutthroats and Galindo in viscera. The drug-lord's body heaved and his breakfast came up in a soupy vomit. It splattered the ground and covered his already dirty shoes.

Holding back their laughter, the solders watched as the remaining insects turned and vanished into the jungle. Their bodies trembled with fear as they retreated, following the paths they had already created and leaving trails of blood and guts.

"Can't believe that actually worked!" Ward said as Muldoon and Gilman engulfed him in bear-hugs and pats.

Gilman laughed, "Well, believe it, Doc!"

"Fucking Bug-Killer you are," Muldoon added with his own laugh. Then he paused. "Fuck… wonder if we'll meet one in an Edgar-suit."

Carter walked up behind the three soldiers and gave the back of Muldoon's head a firm back-handed slap. The man winced, then turned. "One of these days," Carter said in a soft, threatening voice, "your big fat mouth is going to get you in trouble."

"True," Muldoon said with that smile still plastered on his face, "but when that day comes, you'll be right there to say 'Fucking told ya so'."

"Enough," Armitage said as he motioned for Ward. "Have a break. Check your gear and be ready to move out in ten… Chuck, this itches like a bitch."

As the medic went over to deal with Armitage, the remaining members of The Cutthroats found spots on the ground to sit and relax. Muldoon monitored Galindo as he broke down the HK417 with a precision that sent a shiver down the drug-lord's spine.

The others were already busy relaxing, which was the first rule; any chance to get some rest, take it.

"Well," Gilman said with no preamble, "I think we can safely say this mission is buggered."

"Fucked," Nightingale corrected the man with a typical thunder-like rumble. He leaned against a tree trunk and closed his eyes.

Randolph Carter flopped down next to Muldoon and glared at Galindo. "I wouldn't go that far," he said while tearing open a field ration. "I'd say 'fucked seven ways from Friday'." Carter's pale eyes bore into the prisoner and the Mexican flinched. The Captain rubbed his bald head then smiled, which made Galindo look away.

"Still," Gilman persisted in keeping the conversation going, "betcha it doesn't get as bad as Siberia."

Before anyone could tell the man to shut his mouth, Armitage cried out in pain. The five men looked over and Galindo turned pale. With the bandage removed, the wound Henry Armitage had sustained was clear; the outer edges of the cavity were brown and burnt from the heat of the bullet. Pieces of skin hung loosely from under the brow and the skin just under the large hole was slack. Inside the empty socket, dark red muscles pulsed and twitched with sense memory movements and lengths of cream nerve branches could be seen.

Ward dabbed gently with disinfected cotton and whistled. "Fuck me, boss," he said, impressed beyond belief, "any other man would be on the ground howling for their mum's tits."

"I'm not any man," Armitage growled, then grunted from the pain. "How bad is it?"

Muldoon chuckled, "You're finally gonna be handsome, boss! Just like me."

The men laughed at the joke, and Armitage casually gave him the bird. His middle finger trembled slightly, which was to be expected after all they had been through. But when the Major saw Galindo's interested expression, he lowered it then said, "Get it cleaned up best you can. But I'm not wearing gauze for the rest of the mission."

Charles Dexter Ward shook his head. "Good to know your sense of humour wasn't damaged," he said as his hand went in to his pack. A second later he pulled out a black rolled-up piece of leather.

"Ta," Armitage said as he placed the eye-patch around his face. "Fucking any of you call me Snake, not even the ants will find you."

At the mention of the bugs, the men went silent. For a moment they had forgotten the gigantic insects. Galindo's eyes darted about, scanning the area for signs of the monsters.

"What the fuck with those things?" Ward said as he and Armitage joined the men. "You'd think David Attenborough would've talked about them, right?"

Carter turned, his head slowly cocking to the side, and stared at the medic; the look of disbelief at the stupidity of the statement made Muldoon giggle and Armitage roll his eyes. They all knew what was coming next.

"What?" Ward said, oblivious to the mounting storm that was about to be unleashed on him. "He would've done so, right?"

Carter pinched the bridge of his nose and spoke slowly, in the same way a parent would to an especially slow child. "Charles," he said using the man's proper name, "how, just how the fuck could you believe that the BBC would ever find out about this place?" He rubbed his head again, "Explain to me, please. Explain how if not even General Carpenter knew about this place, a British TV Channel could know? Tell me, for the love of all that is right in this world. Tell me!"

At the mention of Carpenter, Jorge Galindo's eyes lit up, and the man fought to not smile. Quickly, he lowered his head and hoped nobody saw the moment of hope that crossed his face.

Unfortunately for the criminal, the leader of The Cutthroats did.

"Oi!" Armitage called to the man. "You got something to say? Share with the group," his voice was inviting but with a slight edge to it.

Instantly the others went quiet and looked at the now anxious Galindo. His eyes darted from man to man and his face was one of guilt. "I don't know anything," he said, trying to sound innocent.

The Major shook his head. "Try again," he said. "It doesn't matter what you think you know about anyone waiting for you. What I want to know is all the intel you have on The Valley of Bicho."

"Valley?" Galindo said, rolling the word around his mouth. "What is 'Valley'?"

"Where we are right now," he said helpfully. "This place with the giant ants…" his voice went silent from the death stare Carter gave him. He smiled weakly and mouthed the word 'sorry' before checking his ammunition.

Jorge Galindo nodded, "El Valle de Bicho," he said in a solemn tone that gave the situation gravitas. "Todo lo que sé son los cuentos de los guardianes del valle. Los bichos. ¡Ni una sola vez pensé que fueran reales! Mi mama y mi abuela lo hicieron—"

"Thanks, shut the fuck up," Carter said as he shoved the ball-gag back into the man's mouth.

Galindo glared, then spat the gag back out. The ball bounced on the ground and rolled to a stop next to Nightingale's leg. "¡Cómo te atreves! Soy Jorge Galindo y—"

"Please be quiet or I'll put this somewhere guaranteed to keep your mouth shut," Nightingale rumbled as he held up the gag. Slowly he opened his eyes then turned them to the man, the stare unnerving as hell and Gelindo trembled.

"Is it just me," Muldoon said casually, as if the giant's comment had never happened, "or does anyone else have a distinct feeling of… Fuck, I don't know how to describe it."

"Oddness?" Gilman said with a slow nod, for he too felt it.

Nightingale rumbled, "Strangeness? Like we're in a Lovecraftian tale of otherworldliness." He looked at his brothers-in-arms then shook his head, "Why is it hard to believe that I read?"

"It isn't because you're almost the spitting image of Andre the Giant. That's for sure," Muldoon said with a polite smile. "But you are certainly right there."

Carter nodded, checked his watch and stood. He stretched and as the bones popped in his back and arms, the Captain said, "Too bloody right, and I for one don't want to see how fucked this gets. Move out!"

CHAPTER NINE

"Think we'll find any others?" Muldoon asked as he stepped through a puddle. The water filled his boots, and he felt the mosquitoes attack his exposed skin. "At least these are normal sized," he said before shoving Galindo forward again.

The drug-lord stumbled, turned and glared at the man. There was something in his eyes that took the soldier back and he raised his M4A1. "You got something to say?"

Galindo shook his head before turning and continuing his trek. His movements were easier, more fluid as he ducked and weaved through the dense foliage. To the sniper it seemed like he had been born in the jungle, or at least lived here most of his life.

"Boss," he said softly, "I think we better monitor the package. There's something about him that's off."

Carter turned and looked at the man. "You're just saying that because he likes you," he said, then looked to his right. Gilman and Ward walked together. The two younger members of the team had a brotherly bond unlike the others, and it made him smile. "Oi, lovers," he said. "Eyes forward. Nothing is gonna sneak up on us. Got it?"

Ward didn't answer, he nodded and jogged past the man until he was on the left flank. "Boss, if you need a rest, don't be afraid to speak up."

"No fucking chance," Armitage said as he checked the map. They were still a-ways from the EVAC zone, but at the pace they were travelling he was positive they'd make it on time. "We continue pushing until there is no chance of any other nasty surprises. Or traps," he added with a glance at Galindo.

"The legends say the guardians are hormigas. Nothing else, promise," the drug-lord said with a genuine smile. But there was something behind his eyes that Armitage didn't like.

"Hank," Nightingale's voice was subdued and with the deepness it came through as a sub-sonic rumble, "You better come and see this."

Armitage sighed. "Carter, any trouble, kneecap the package," he said before jogging up towards the point man.

The five men watched their TL disappear into the green, and Randolph Carter looked at Galindo. "Why are you still here? In the fracas earlier, you could've gone walkabout without any trouble. What gives?"

It was a question the men had had since they escaped the ants, and it had only been a matter of time until one built up the nerves to ask it. Luckily for them, Carter had no fear. "Well?" he asked again, and his drill-Sargent voice showed.

"No podría saber lo que estás insinuando," Galindo said with an air of indifference. He continued to follow the path Gilman and Ward created. The two soldiers followed the trail left by both Nightingale and Armitage. As he moved, the drug-lord paused for a second and looked to the treetops; his eyes filled with concern and they looked like he was watching for something. "Should we keep moving?"

"Why?" Muldoon said as he stood a meter behind the man. "What's got your knickers in a twist?" his eyes followed the man's gaze, and he smiled. "Don't tell me we're in the home of giant flies?"

As Galindo opened his mouth, Carter's voice cut him off. "Keep him moving," the Captain snarled. "We need to catch up to Hank and Sammy. Double time it, now!"

"Don't bellow in my ear," Armitage said into the comms as he slowed to a stop and his eyes went wide.

The fresh air whipping around his face was cooling, and it made him feel a moment of peace, a rare moment for the man, but it was momentary. His mind reeled from the sight before him, and Sam Nightingale's face broke into a gigantic smile.

"Fuck me in the ass," Armitage mumbled as he stared at the open sky and the sheer drop before him.

The giant laughed, "Buy me dinner first… Or a bottle of Giaconda Chardonnay." The smile quickly vanished and the communications officer said, "Hank, that's not the problem."

Armitage shook his head as he looked down; it had to be at least a two-hundred meter drop until they hit the crystal clear blue water of the raging river. It wasn't on the map, which meant the intel the local authorities had given Carpenter was outdated or wrong on purpose.

"What is?" he asked, even though he didn't really want to know. And the sudden buzzing in his ear didn't help in the least.

Turning, he saw Nightingale standing next to a pile of faded leather. The giant used the barrel of his carbine to hold up a length of the material; shards of light leaked through it, and the bumps and grooves of the discarded skin sent a shudder of dread through the Major.

"Don't tell me we've got giant snakes too?" the one-eyed man asked as the rest of his team and the drug-lord emerged from the jungle.

Nightingale shook his head. "Honestly, no fucking idea," he said, then looked at Ward. "Doc, any ideas?"

Ward huffed and puffed from the exertion mixed with the overwhelming humidity. "Why is it always me?" he said as he stalked over to the shed skin. "I'm a doctor of human anatomy. Humans! Not fucking insects."

"Yeah," Carter said as he crouched next to the edge of the cliff, "but out of all of us, you're the smartest." His eyes studied the cliff-face and his mind began working overtime. There was no straightforward way for them to get down, let alone cross the river. The bald man frowned as his ears picked up a deep humming. Carter shook his head. He was probably tired, and it was his mind playing tricks on him.

Either way, he needed to focus and get everyone safely down

the side of the cliff. He shrugged before looking over to the collection of men.

Ward pushed past Gilman and Galindo without a word. His face was locked in an expression of annoyance at always being summoned. The moment he saw what the men were studying, the annoyed look morphed into one of intrigue.

Nightingale and Armitage held the shabby, golden-coloured hunk of leather. The two men still did not understand what it was, and the many folds showed whatever had created it was massive.

"Spread it out," Ward said with a curt gesture. He shook his head slightly. The deep humming filled the periphery of his hearing.

Carter nudged Galindo. "Get in there," he said before joining The Cutthroats in their new task. The group of men, tired beyond belief though they were, pulled, stretched and used their reservoirs of strength to get the shrivelled, sun-shrunken hunk of leather unfurled.

"Oh, fuck me!" Muldoon said as the men stared in disbelief at the final shape. Around them the air was filled with the humming, now it sounded like a buzzing similar to a chainsaw revving.

"You said it," Armitage said as the men dropped the shed skin. His foot crushed the wax-paper like wing and the Major glared at Galindo. "What else haven't you told us?"

The drug-lord let the large, pointed sucker flop to the ground as he shrugged. Slowly the others followed suit, and the discarded skin slowly crinkled and rolled up into itself. "I've told you all I know," Galindo said, and his voice was nothing but defensive. "But if that is what I think it is… we need to go now!"

"Good luck with that," Carter shouted as the chainsaw-like buzz over-powered their voices. "There's no way down!"

Jorge Galindo turned to the Captain and shook his head. "Only a foreigner would think that," he said in a superior tone that made every one of his captors want to beat the shit out of him. Ignoring the death-stares, he continued speaking, "There is always a way. And I know of one… Follow me!"

Without another word, the drug-lord turned and jogged past the one-eyed man and the giant. The Cutthroats looked at each other and slowly the giant rumbled, "He's being too helpful."

"Yeah, I don't like it," Carter mumbled as the six men turned and followed the Mexican fading from view. "Chuckie, what's the best way to take him down without causing permanent damage?"

"Behave," Armitage growled with a laugh. "The moment he gets us down this shit show, we'll lock him down. Tommy, you and Disney are in charge of him. Got it?"

Muldoon smiled as he pulled out his combat knife. "My pleasure," he said, doing his best Anthony Hopkins impression. "I think he'll go well with a chianti and some—"

"Down!" Gilman bellowed as a large black blur the size of a hangglider swooped down past the men. The Cutthroats dove to the ground and they looked up in time to see the gigantic mosquito bank and turn around. The chainsaw-like roar came from the wings.

It dropped and sped towards the prone men. A slither of clear liquid oozed from the tip of its sucker and dropped to the ground, where it sizzled and singed it.

"Well," Muldoon said as the men rolled out of the way, "now we know where that came from!"

"Stop talking!" Armitage shouted as he readied his M4A1. "I'll provide cover while you get to Galindo! Don't let him get down without any of you!" Raising the rifle, the Major peered through the scope and squeezed the trigger.

A series of holes appeared in the right wing and the mosquito shrieked before dropping out of the sky. The moment it thudded to the ground, it began thrashing about and crying as blood oozed from the gouges and gashes it gave itself; dirt and branches punctured the soft flesh and pulled the legs and thorax open.

"Move the fuck out, NOW!" Armitage shouted as he stalked over to the downed bug. He placed a boot on the sucker and fired. The bullets shredded the head in a cascade of gunfire and blood. The gun clicked empty and in a smooth motion, Henry Armitage reloaded his carbine.

Behind him, he heard the pounding of his men's boots as they ran after Galindo. *'Bout fucking time,* he thought as five more of the monsters appeared in the distance. *Fuck this for a laugh,* Armitage thought as he turned and quickly caught up with the others.

CHAPTER TEN

"What's the fucking hold-up?" the Major demanded. "You planning a picnic?" He glared at the five men who made up his team. Each of them was looking down and none heard him. Looking back, he saw the fast approaching mosquitoes. They had to get moving. "What the fuck is it?"

Carter pointed and his friend looked down, following his finger; Galindo was scrambling down the cliff face! He used a series of ledges and hand-holds that were manmade, but the man moved deftly and with no problems. "You first," the Captain said as he stepped aside.

"Sure thing," Armitage said as once again the air was filled with the chainsaw-sounding roar. "I'll let you drongos handle this!" he said before lowering himself over the edge.

Captain Randolph Carter's eyes widened at the sight of his commanding officer rapidly clambering down the side of the cliff. Even with his impressive frame, the man moved with grace and ease. He matched each of the hand-holds and foot placements of Galindo. "Fuck, he's good."

"It's why they pay him the medium-sized bucks," Muldoon said as he looked up and spotted the mosquitoes. "Eyes open, boys."

"What's the time?" Nightingale asked as his hand gripped the handle of his own carbine.

Muldoon raised his M4A1 before saying, "Five, but I wouldn't be surprised if it was closer to six or seven."

Carter spun while his finger held in the trigger. "Love your counting ability," he said as his weapon spewed bullets. In the distance, the monsters dodged and weaved, avoiding the hunks of death speeding at them.

Muldoon and Nightingale followed suit, each of them aiming at the most open and alone creature. Unfortunately, their distance made their shots almost useless, all they could do was keep the beasts at bay.

Ward shoved Gilman, who stumbled before starting his own descent. He sweated profusely and his hands, even though they were clad in gloves, slipped slightly on the hard dust rocks. With a shake of his head, Charles Dexter Ward dropped out of sight, his own movements smooth and precise.

"Get moving," Carter ordered as he continued firing in short bursts. "I'll hold them off best as I can—"

"No heroics," Muldoon countered as he vanished below the ledge. The two remaining men heard his grunts and a gasp. "They're heading down!"

The sniper was right; the mosquitoes had spotted the trail of men moving down the cliff-face and had changed course accordingly. As they dove their wings, dipping slightly to propel them towards their prey, the chainsaw sound turned into a motorbike growl.

The way each of the mosquitoes dipped and bobbed through the air, now wary of the attacks the meal-to-be had, it reminded the six soldiers of fighter-planes.

"Move your asses!" Carter bellowed as he and Nightingale did their best to catch up. The two men knew that it was a numbers game and the moment they touched the water, they'd be home free. "You've got incoming."

Far below the six soldiers, Jorge Galindo looked up. The screaming and almost continuous rain of dust and rocks made it harder and harder to focus on his hands and feet. One wrong move and he'd fall, tumbling to his death until the rocks greeted him.

At the sight of the mosquitoes, the drug-lord's eyes went wide, and he shouted, "Don't let them touch you!"

"No fucking shit!" Muldoon shouted down as he fired his handgun. The Kimber kicked wildly and the closest bug dodged the bullets easily. "Fuck you very much!" the sniper growled as he continued his descent.

"Save your ammo!" Armitage ordered while slashing at one of the flying menaces. The blade of his knife made contact and sliced open its stinger.

With a wail of pain, the mosquito spun and the Major stabbed the bulbous, fat red-filled abdomen.

They heard a tiny pop, then a long stream of blood spurted out and directly at the Major. Armitage clenched his mouth shut as the noxious liquid covered him, showering him from head to toe in the bug's food.

His foot slipped from the wetness and the one-eyed man felt the world leave him. He was floating, and the entirety of his being knew he'd be dead and joining the now falling dead mosquito.

With nothing else to do, he closed his eye and smiled. His team would make it, they had all the training and nothing could stop them. Not even these fucking bugs!

"Gotcha!" Nightingale exclaimed as his hand, the size of Armitage's head, engulfed the Major's arm.

Armitage felt the world snap back and his feet landed on solid rock. Opening his eye, he saw the giant and all he could say was, "You're a fucking saint!"

"Just call me Mother Teresa," Sam Nightingale said with a smile that turned into a worried frown.

The men stopped, a panicked cry filled their ears, and they looked up.

Walter Gilman's left arm and leg kicked out wildly at two of the flying insects. They dodged and weaved, doing what they could to get as close as possible to the man. The two other mosquitoes watched. They hovered off to the side and waited to see if their brothers would be successful.

Each frantic kick did nothing but to make the bugs move and close-in. Gilman's eyes were wide with panic and he frothed at the mouth. "Help me!" he squealed as his right hand lost its grip and the man fell with a high-pitched scream of horror.

"Disney!" Muldoon cried out as he changed course and moved towards the falling man. He winced and tears welled up as his brother-in-arms tumbled, bouncing off the rocks with each hit, leaving trails of blood and layers of skin.

There was nothing they could do to save the man. All they could do was watch as one mosquito swooped down, taking the chance to feed.

A loud wet thud echoed through the ravine and the cliff trembled from the impact of the mosquito impaling Walter Gilman. The sucker embedded in the man's stomach worked, and the air was filled with the rancid smell of burning flesh.

"Jesus fuck! Tommy! Please help me! Please! Randy! Shit! Help me! Oh, God!" Gilman begged and cried as he felt an overpowering suction and pressure build up in his body. It was unlike anything the soldier had felt in his entire life, and all he knew was immeasurable pain. Everything was coming undone and all the energy was being torn from his self.

The moment his stomach and intestines shifted, Gilman knew what was happening, and he howled in agony. His insides were ripped and sucked from their places; the intestines unravelled as they travelled up the long translucent tube, the other men staring in terror and distress as Gilman's stomach erupted and the acidic juices flowed, mingling with dark red blood.

As the gigantic mosquito continued to suck and suck, more and more of the man's internal organs shot up the tube into the waiting monster's hungry belly. Gilman's body slowly deflated, all of his juices and liquids; blood, bodily juices and semen were drained, his flesh shrunk from the vacuum. His screams became hoarse until it turned into an inhuman groan. Both dark eyes rolled back into his head before being sucked back into his head with a squelch.

"We've got to do something!" Muldoon shouted as he lifted the M4A1 high into the air. His armed swayed wildly as he tried to aim at the attacking creature.

Carter couldn't move, he was frozen in place but his voice cracked like lightning. "STAND THE FUCK DOWN! DISNEY IS DEAD!"

He was right and at the same time he said the word 'dead', the six men heard a terrible ripping sound as cracks formed all over the trembling man's body.

Walter Gilman's skin vanished in a spurt of blood as it was pulled from the man's body and up into the mosquito's belly. Drying red and blue muscles danced on the frame of bones, and the hideous rictus grin stopped Muldoon cold.

He watched, uncomprehending, as the mosquito backed away, the limp skinless body flailing about on the sucker. With a violent shake of its head, the mosquito launched the corpse into the air and all watched it tumble into the distance.

"Kill it!" Armitage ordered while raising his weapon. He didn't wait for the order to be obeyed. He felt nothing but a white hot rage. He'd failed his men. It was Siberia all over again and there was nothing he could do about it.

The burst of fire echoed throughout the ravine and filled the men's ears with the staccato sound of fireworks.

The wings of the mosquito, sucker dripping with blood, were shredded into tattered remains from the shots. It hovered for a second, wings flapping in futility before it fell from the sky, tumbling into the raging water below that swallowed it without a care.

As one, the other three insects turned their attention on the men and it looked like they were glaring. Each of the flying menaces had their heads angled down slightly and the eyes curved in, just like a human's death stare.

"Think they're made," Carter said as he adjusted his hand-hold and footing. There was no way he'd let them knock him off and fall to his death. As his left hand tightened its grip, the right readied his carbine for the incoming assault. "Aim for the wings," he growled.

Putting aside their grief at the loss of Gilman, The Cutthroats all took out their M4A1s and raised them. Jorge Galindo looked stricken with panic and the certainty he'd be dead soon.

Armitage saw the man's eyes darting between the armed soldiers and the hovering monsters. "Jorge," he said, trying his best to make his voice sound soothing, "keep climbing down. We'll follow you—"

"¡No puede ser!" the man spat as the air was once again filled with the deep machine-like roar of the mosquitoes.

The three flying bugs dove, the wings propelling them faster than before, and the five men opened fire. This time they didn't bother to fire in the standard controlled bursts. They were out for revenge and wanted to make these hellspawn pay for taking one of their own.

As the bullets whizzed through the air, the mosquitoes weaved and dodged them easily.

Ward's carbine rifle clicked empty, but the man kept his finger pressed down on the trigger. Next to him, Nightingale slowed the rate of his own firing, his finger easing off the trigger every second until he had a good line on the closest mosquito.

"Fucking mozzies," the giant rumbled as he exhaled gently while he squeezed the trigger. The carbine kicked slightly and coughed, spewing the bullets at the flying monster.

The left wing crumpled from the assault and then it spun out of control, shrieking before smashing into the cliff-face with a splat, face first. The speed and bulk of the mosquito squashed the sucker up into the face, and the inertia kept it going. As it continued into the hard rocks, the pressure of the impact pushed everything until the slim body couldn't handle it.

Ward and Nightingale watched, enormous smiles on their faces as the mosquito's body split open before exploding in a shower of blood, organs and the decomposing remains of its previous meals.

"This ain't a movie!" Carter's voice snapped the two men out of their stupor. "Reload and keep firing!"

"Yessir!" Ward said as his hands moved on their own and he quickly got another clip locked and loaded. Ignoring the warm wetness sliding down the back of his neck, Charles Dexter Ward squeezed the trigger again.

Armitage looked down. The drug-lord was scrambling down without a care, and it looked as if he would fall at any second. "Move out," he said into the comms as he started his descent, trying to match the same speed and placement of Galindo.

Slowly the men climbed down, their focus torn between not falling to their dooms and the two remaining mosquitoes, who had withdrawn and hovered, planning their next move.

All but Muldoon moved down the cliff-face. The team's sniper's eyes were dead and his arm hung limp. Without thinking, he pulled out a frag grenade, yanked the pin and bellowed, "Suck on this, you cunts!"

Carter looked up in time to see the throw. His eyes went wide and before he could shout out to the man, the explosive device sailed through the air towards the mosquitoes.

One of the bugs spun and used its bulbous stomach to knock the grenade back at the man, like it was playing a deranged game of tennis.

"Move! Fucking move!" Randolph Carter shouted at the same time the frag grenade exploded, sending rocks and debris raining down on the frantically scrambling men.

Long cracks formed, spider webbing out across the rough surface. The rumbling and vibrations stopped the five men cold, and they looked up in horror; the cliff-face shifted and gigantic slabs of rock fell.

"Drop!" Armitage bellowed before letting go.

CHAPTER ELEVEN

Muldoon coughed and spluttered, trying to rid his body of the invasive water threatening to drown him. His body felt five times too heavy and a part of his brain told him to just close his eyes and let everything go.

He felt something hard and large smack into him and his eyes opened. Nightingale glared at him while smiling. “Good,” he rumbled as his legs kicked, keeping the two men afloat, “the Major will be happy to kick your ass personally.”

Tommy Muldoon laughed as his legs worked. He wouldn’t die, not today and especially not in the middle of this godforsaken jungle. “This is fucking heavy!” he shouted as his hands tried to remove the combat vest and his pack.

“Head for the shore!” Armitage’s voice came through the earpieces garbled, but the command was clear. Nightingale and Muldoon used the momentum from the river to leap above the waterline.

“Boss!” Muldoon shouted as he was dragged under the water. The force of the water was almost too much for him, but the massive tree-trunk-like legs kicking next to him gave the man something to work with.

“The shore is about ten meters to the right!” he gasped the

moment his face was above water.

Further down, the two saw the rest of the squad fighting against the currents; Ward and Armitage were close to each other, they had come up with the same idea and were doing all they could to stay above water. He couldn't see Carter or Galindo. "Eyes on the package?" he said while spitting water.

Henry Armitage fought against the water as his mind worked faster than it ever had before. *How the fuck had the mission gone from bad to worse to fucked in a matter of hours?* he thought as he kicked with all he had, which wasn't much. The Major knew of men who had drowned or almost done so and that it felt like going home or slipping into a warm bed. Each time he was dragged under and the water rushed into his lungs, the only thing Armitage felt was panic wash over him and the sensation of a slow death.

Next to him, Ward struggled to pull himself and his commanding officer over to the river bank. Each time he kicked and pulled against the current and raging water, it pushed back, sending the two men under. The old saying, two steps forward, one step back crossed his mind, and he chuckled.

"Make for me!" Carter's voice was hoarse, and it got the attention of the almost drowned men. They looked over to see him and an unconscious Galindo lying on a massive, relatively flat rock formation.

"Of fucking course," Muldoon muttered as he and Nightingale stopped struggling and let the current sweep them to the grinning man.

Armitage tugged on the medic's shoulder and pointed to Carter. "Fuck yeah!" Ward said as he stopped fighting and the two careened towards safety.

Randolph Carter grinned, the smile threatening to slice his face in half as he helped pull Ward up and out of the river. The moment the medic felt dry land, he collapsed and began heaving, expelling the noxious and dirty water from his lungs. "You're okay;" Carter said reassuringly while slapping the man's back.

"Little help, if you don't mind!" Armitage said as his hands slipped on the slick wet rock. His boots couldn't find purchase and what little strength he had was fading fast, and he knew that the moment he went back under, it'd be game over.

"Not so fast," the rumble of Nightingale's voice filled his ears as the massive man lifted him up. The Major scrambled, trying his best not to kick out, and he ignored the feeling of being a child again.

Armitage coughed and wheezed as the sun warmed his face and started drying his clothes and equipment. Without his bidding, his eye closed, and he focused on his breathing and the sounds of his men getting safe.

Muldoon huffed and puffed, then looked at Nightingale. "How the fuck can you lift him?" he asked while pointing at Armitage.

"Wasn't easy!"

Carter cleared his throat, and the two men stopped their talking. The Captain looked at Muldoon and quietly asked, "Just what in the flying fuck did you think you were doing?"

Tommy Muldoon opened his mouth, but the bald man continued to speak.

"What could possibly have possessed that pea-sized brain of yours to throw a frag at an enemy who can fucking-fly!" Carter didn't pause for breath as he continued berating the man. "Out of all the dumb-fucking-ass things you've ever said or done, this, THIS, has to be top of the fucking list!" he pointed to the unconscious Galindo. "Because of you, now we have to fucking wait for the mother-fucking package to wake the fuck up, because believe you me, I am NOT carrying his sorry ass across the—"

"He's going to be fine," Ward said. He had the Mexican's head in his hands and was gingerly inspecting it. "No lacerations. His breathing is normal, I'd say he just took in too much water," he placed his head on the man's chest then nodded. "Yeah, he's fine."

"Fan-fucking-tastic," Armitage said, rubbing his eye. He sat up with a groan and stared at Muldoon. "Tom, seriously, what the fuck? You're a professional, act like one!"

Tommy Muldoon said nothing. He felt the stares and knew his brothers-in-arms were looking at him. "Yeah," he said after a second. "I fucked up. But you saw what that thing did to Disney!"

"Yeah," Carter said, and his voice softened. "We all saw what happened. But, just like what Hank said, you're a fucking professional! You don't fly off the handle and put the rest of us at fucking risk!"

"I know!" Muldoon shouted as water splashed up, soaking him further. "I fucking know… What do you want me to say? Yeah, I fucked up but—"

The man screamed as he slipped and fell backwards straight into the water. Within seconds, Tommy Muldoon vanished beneath the raging rapids. At the same time, Jorge Galindo coughed hard and opened his eyes.

"It's a fucking miracle," Armitage said while he rolled the drug-lord onto his back. "Sam. You and Randy get in and find Tommy. We're not letting this fucking place take another of us."

The two splashes that followed gave the Major a small sense of relief. Galindo grunted, then cried out as his arms were roughly yanked behind him. The thick heavy-duty cable-tie cuffs that slid up around his wrists cut into the skin. "That fucking hurt!"

Armitage pulled the man up and whispered into his ear, "Good. Enjoy it. What waits for you in the next life will be a million times worse than this. I guaran-fucking-tee it."

Galindo looked back and smiled. It was a chilling sight and instinctively the Major stepped back. "No hay nada que puedas decir o amenazarme con eso, sería peor que lo que he visto o hecho," the man said, and his voice was ice cold.

Ignoring the man, Ward muttered to himself, "Hope Randy and Sammy are having more fun."

Carter and Nightingale swam, their tired legs propelling them through the water as their legs screamed for them to stop and rest. Each breath taken burned, and the men pushed away thoughts of Muldoon drowning or being swept too far downstream.

Neither spoke as they powered on. They couldn't risk letting any more of the unclean water into their bodies. All they knew was that they had to get Muldoon and then reach the shoreline and wait for the rest.

Fucking easy.

Randolph Carter couldn't believe their actual luck when he felt the hand wrap around his leg. Reaching into the water he felt the wrist and the forearm; it had to be Muldoon.

Fucking-A, he thought as he pulled the man up from the depths. Around him, Nightingale splashed, but the water had calmed and was now flowing normally.

Muldoon's face exploded from the surface with an almighty gasp for air. He took deep breaths, struggling to breathe and take in the precious oxygen he needed so badly.

The two men were splashed by the massive ripples caused by Nightingale, who laughed as he grabbed the two men. He kept them floating as he kicked towards the riverbank.

"Report," Armitage's voice sounded distant through the comms. "Did you get the dumb-cunt?"

Carter chuckled, "Yeah, we got the fuckwit. Water's calm down here. Will make it easier to get to shore."

They heard three splashes and Muldoon whispered, "Can we have a swim, Randy? It's nice at the beach this time of the year."

Before the Captain could answer, Nightingale frowned then pointed. "What the hell is that?"

Turning, the two men saw something long, thick, black and wet cut through the water straight for them. Its tube-like shape was unlike anything the men had seen and its way of moving, using the ripples of the water to pull itself, was mesmerising.

"Whatever it is," Carter said with an edge to his voice, "I don't like it." He clicked his comms, "Beware. There is something in the water and it's coming right for us."

"Copy that," Armitage's voice sounded closer than before. He, Ward, and the prisoner must've already reached the calm water. "We're almost at you. Don't engage, just get to the shore and out of the water. We're right behind you."

"Like always," Muldoon said as his arms worked and he tread the water. "Let's do what he says and get the fuck out of the—"

Nightingale yelped as he was dragged under the water. The black tube wrapped itself around his torso and his brothers watched the underwater struggle.

The Captain watched, his eyes darting about, studying the rapid movements of the struggling pair. As he continued to stare, he didn't notice the other black tube creep up behind him. Nor did he feel it slowly wrap around him.

"Randy," Muldoon said right before the Captain was dragged under the water too. The sniper continued treading water as he looked about and hoped there wasn't a third one.

Beneath the waterline, Carter and Nightingale fought to escape the tightening coil of their attackers. Each time they pushed away with their arms, the lower coil gripped tighter and tighter, cutting off the blood to their legs. If they kicked out, the coil wrapped around their chest, squeezed and the air was forced out of their lungs.

As their eyes filled with water mixed with a stinging sensation neither man could get a good look at the new terror assaulting them. From what they could grip and dig their fingers into, the fresh horror's flesh was leathery and soft and seemed to go on forever, a constant pressure that would never let them go.

Blackness formed on the edge of Nightingale's vision and he struggled against the urge to open his mouth and suck in the air that wasn't there. At the same time, he saw the head of the tube rise up and the mouth open to reveal rows and rows of sharp teeth. It was a leech!

Weakly, the man raised his right hand to try and stop the gaping maw from engulfing his head and sucking him until he was dead. But his strength failed him, and the leech attacked.

A sharp stabbing pain across his shoulder and upper-arm forced the giant to open his eyes while the tight coils around his body loosened. Floating, leaking blood was the leech; large knife gashes and wounds covered its body, and the man felt the world surge as he was pulled back to the surface and the land of the living.

CHAPTER TWELVE

"You're one lucky bastard," Ward said with a sigh of relief. Lying on the ground under his gaze, Sam Nightingale blinked and coughed, then turned to his side and brought up the water from his lungs.

Next to the communications officer, Randolph Carter sat up and heaved. His entire body ached all over and he was positive his ribs were not cracked but broken. Each breath made him wince, and the medic placed a hand on his shoulder. "I'm fine," Carter wheezed. "Let me rest for a moment."

Ward looked at his commanding officer. Armitage had his Kimber Gold out and had it lazily pointed at Galindo.

The drug-lord sat on the mid-point where the sand was dry and wet and glared at the one-eyed man. There was something about the way he held himself that hinted at an unseen well of passion just waiting to be unleashed.

"Boss, think we can have a break and catch our breath?" Ward asked as he slumped to the sand next to Carter. "I'm completely buggered."

"Yeah!" Muldoon said. He struggled to his feet and continued speaking. "Aren't we going to say a word for Disney? Or those fucking things in the water?" He spun and pointed a trembling

M4A1 at the Mexican. “What other wonders of the animal world are we going to fucking encounter? Those were fucking leeches! Leeches! And my best friend… my brother, is gone.”

With a loud sob the man dropped to his knees burying his face into his hands and his words were a slap to The Cutthroats’ faces. In their rush to survive, the euphoria that came from a gun-fight Henry Armitage, Sam Nightingale, Randolph Carter and Charles Dexter Ward had all but forgotten their fallen brother. Now, to see Muldoon, the resident comedian of the team, openly weeping and mourning the loss of their own, it provided a sobering effect.

Armitage sighed and stood. His body ached, but there was nothing he could do about it. The mission wasn’t over yet, and until they got Galindo on the EVAC helicopter, there was no time to dawdle.

“Tommy,” he said, letting his emotions fill his voice, “Disney will be missed. Like all of our departed brothers, we’ll drink to their memories and deeds at the clubhouse and one day we’ll be together—”

“Don’t say ‘Valhalla’,” Muldoon said with a snarl that stopped the Major dead in his tracks. The sniper’s face was contorted into an expression of pure anguish and rage and he spat, “Disney’s gone! And that’s it! He is dead and gone and there is nothing else after. No heaven. No, hell and no fucking Valhalla!”

His cry echoed across the shoreline, and the lapping of the water filled the silence left by the man’s outburst.

The team leader’s shoulders slumped, and he sank back to the sand. Next to him, Galindo chuckled and shook his head.

“Something funny?” Carter asked while he flashed the man a sublime death stare.

Galindo’s smile never left his face. “You are funny,” he drawled, enunciating each word. “Weeping over the death of a killer. It’s the greatest form of hypocrisy,” he laughed then went quiet.

There was something about the way he spoke that held the attention of the men, except for Muldoon. The sniper had his head in his hands and was sobbing quietly.

“You want to talk about hypocrisy?” Ward asked with his own smirk. “You? The great and powerful ‘El Dandy’! You, who’s ordered the deaths of countless men, women and children. You dare to talk to us about hypocrisy?"

"I do," Galindo answered without a moment's pause. "Because unlike you and your kind, every death I've ordered has weighed heavily on my immortal soul," his voice shook with rage and sadness, but the man continued to speak. "How about you? How many men have you taken everything away from since you put on that uniform? And not just today but your entire careers?"

It was a question none of the soldiers had ever actually thought about, let alone answered. Who could've guessed that a Mexican drug-lord would be the one to ask? Not The Cutthroats, that was for sure.

"It doesn't matter," Nightingale rumbled. "What does is that we carry on and do our jobs."

Jorge Galindo didn't bother to hide his laughter. It sounded strange coming from their prisoner, and it made the team members uncomfortable. "What sort of pendejo are you to say that? Do you actually believe that? Or is it something drilled into you during basic training?"

"All. None. Fuck you," Carter said as he turned away from the Mexican. This was a conversation they couldn't waste valuable time on. His eyes went to the blood-covered dog-tags his fist clenched around.

Galindo snorted, "The answer of a true war dog. Do your master's bidding, don't ask questions and get a treat and a belly rub." He shook his head, amazed at the way these men spoke and worked.

"What about you?" Armitage asked in a voice full of curiosity and frustration. He didn't look at the man but kept his eyes on the map. Somehow it had survived not only the fall but the dunk in the water. "How many have you killed?"

"Too many to remember them all," the drug-lord said, "and that is my burden to carry." The way he spoke, it sounded like he was truly remorseful of his actions, "Same as when my boys are taken, raped, tortured, then killed. Their blood is on my hands, mine alone."

"Boo-fucking-hoo," Muldoon said, and his voice was muffled. "You want our sympathy? Life is nothing but blood and death.

Survival of the fittest and all that shit!"

The drug-lord said nothing as his eyes went from soldier to soldier; each had the same look of agreement mixed with a weariness only seen in the elderly or hardened killers from a pulp story. For Galindo though, there was something else that the men holding him captive hadn't even considered and was something no-man from the first world could.

He opened his mouth and spoke slowly at first, letting his words wash over the five men. "You are right. Life is nothing but blood and death. But tell me if you've known it all your lives? Were you born into it, or did you seek it out as a way to have some excitement in your worthless lives?"

"Little bit of column A. Little bit of column B," Ward said with a shrug.

"For me," Galindo said with a small sad smile, "I was born into it. As are nearly all Mexicans. My country's history is nothing but bloodshed and you, 'civilised' men come in trying to tell us how to live? You know nothing about survival! Every single moment of my life has been nothing but that struggle. This, this life I've created which you all deem to be worse than a politician or a zorra, is all I have. All I could do. That or die poor and forgotten."

The Cutthroats listened intently as the Mexican continued his survey. They had to admit that he had a point, though his reasoning was rocky at best.

"If that's so," Armitage said without looking up from the map, "then shouldn't Mexico be a country of Narcos?"

Galindo snorted and his voice took on the tone of a politician, "Your logic is childish. We've known nothing except violence, from the Mayans and Aztecs to the Spanish Conquest and then up to your 'War on Drugs'. You wouldn't believe what I've had to do to survive."

"Try us," Carter said with a yawn. He'd heard this kind of speech before in movies, but even in real life it sounded hackneyed and rehearsed.

This was what the drug-lord wanted to hear. He smiled again and opened his mouth. "You've read the file the DEA made about me? The way I took control of this empire. Nothing compared to what I had to do before. Prostitution. Not women, but myself. My familia had no money to buy rice, beans and tortillas but there were those who would pay for my young body."

"Sounds like a Hallmark movie," Carter said with another yawn. "Wake me when you get to the good stuff."

"The good stuff?" Galindo repeated the question with a look of confusion. "My life has no good stuff but this. You mourn that man who has killed more men than any virus. You weep for him," he said with a little nod at Muldoon. "But what about the men whose lives you've taken? Not mine, but all of them? Have you wept for them? Their families? The fact that most will now starve since you've taken away the only income source they had?"

He coughed and shook his head, drops of sweat splattering the ferns with slaps. "How many wives, sisters and daughters have you doomed to become whores just to put food on the table? Do you even care or do you shield your conscience behind 'orders'?"

Silence greeted him, and the man hid his smile behind a cough. The Federales and DEA agents had the same reaction, and Jorge Galindo felt powerful and in control of the situation. There was nothing they could say that he didn't have an answer to.

"Do you?" Nightingale rumbled, and the question hung in the air. "Do you care about all those you've robbed of lives because of your drugs?"

"No," Galindo said, and the honesty in his voice was shocking. "Why should I? If they don't buy my product, then they will from someone else. At least my product is pure and without harmful chemicals. And the important thing is, every single one of my employees are covered by health care and social security. Those men you brutally murdered were my family! Who will pay their families? Who will take care of them when they go to prison or need help? Not the government. Nobody will. Except me."

"Well ain't you a fucking saint," Muldoon said with a scoff. He didn't look at the man but instead focused on the shiny metal Carter held.

Galindo laughed, "Yes. To MY people, I am. You would never understand what it is like to wake up every day and wonder if this is the day I die. Constantly living with that makes one appreciate life and take it by the balls—"

"Enough," Armitage said with a disgruntled grunt. His index finger traced a path on the map and he nodded. "We're wasting enough time as it is and there is no way in fucking hell I'm gonna be stranded here."

Muldoon nodded in agreement. "Boss," he said, pulling out his Kimber Gold, "let me put one in this cunt's knee. He won't be a bother anymore."

"You do and you'll be the one to carry his ass over this fucked-up jungle," Carter said as he stood and pulled the slide back on his M4A1. "You heard the man, we're moving out and going double time!"

CHAPTER THIRTEEN

"I wouldn't touch that," Galindo said as Nightingale reached for a bright pink fruit. The giant froze before staring at the Mexican. "Really," he said, doing his best to sound truthful, "you lay a single finger on it and it's your funeral."

Carter watched Nightingale's face as he internally debated whether to believe the man. It was a sight to behold with the rapid changes of expressions that ran across the communications officer's face; suspicion turned into confusion, which finally ended with resignation as his hand dropped and he continued to trudge through the jungle.

"Go on," Carter said, doing his best to sound tempting. Instead, his voice sounded like a poor-man's impression of Peter Cook.

Sam Nightingale looked down at the man and shook his head. "Why do you want me to die?"

"He's hungry and wants to know whether Galindo's telling the truth," Armitage said as he led the six men. They had been battling the ever-thickening foliage of the Lacandon Jungle and it was obvious to both he, Carter and even Galindo that the men were close to collapsing from fatigue.

The Cutthroats continued to push on, though. Each step was a struggle, but the five trained men would not stop until either their mission was completed, or their decomposing carcasses littered the jungle floor.

"Then there'd be two more bodies for the jungle to claim," Galindo said with a knowing smile that made the soldiers uncomfortable. Without another word he followed the one-eyed Major, leaving Carter and Nightingale to stare at the now ominous looking fruit.

"Would've been better to kneecap the fucker," Muldoon snarled as he passed the men. "Least then we'd have something to laugh about."

He stalked after the others, and the wake of his passing left the other two in shock. Carter looked to Nightingale who shrugged then said, "Grief does strange things to us all."

"Fuck that for a laugh," Carter said as he fell in line with the others. "I'd take him making jokes all-fucking-day over the sullen cunt he's become."

Ward shook his head as he brought up the rear. "Give the man a break, will ya?" he said with all the care of a parent. "I'd like to see you deal with the pain of seeing someone you care about be killed by gigantic monsters."

Nightingale chuckled, then lowered his voice to a gruff grumble. "I wasn't born. I was farted out of the abyss, fully formed and ready for action. Now, get moving before I shove my boot so far up your cloaca, you'll be burping laces for a month!"

Ward erupted into laughter at the obvious impression of the Captain who glared at the two men then smiled maliciously.

"That's good. Real funny," he said, and the moment his voice filled the air, the two men went quiet. "No, keep going. I want to hear more," his eyes darted between the two and he laughed. "Fucking hell mates! You need to lighten the fuck up! Now, double time or I'll feed you to the next bug we come across, bollocks first!"

Over the comms they heard Armitage's voice, "If you're done with the circle-jerk, get the fuck up here!"

The three brothers-in-arms smiled at each other, then jogged quickly, following the trail left by the three others. Each moved with a reinvigorated step as if the moment of bullshitting had brought them back from the brink and they felt ready to take on the world again.

"What's the problem?" Carter said as his eyes darted about, scanning the surrounding vines, trees and bushes.

"This entire fucking job," Muldoon mumbled, then grunted. "Can we just fucking nuke this entire shit-hole? I mean it! I've had enough of feeling the sweat pool in my ass, and I'm more than positive I've got a killer case of swamp-crotch."

"Too much fucking information!" Carter said, laughing at the images popping into his mind.

Ward shook his head and said, "What the fuck is swamp-crotch?"

"Cut the shit and get up here. Now!" Armitage's voice cut through the laughter and mental images popping into the men's minds. The command snapped the men instantly into action, and they charged through the vines and low-hanging branches without a care.

The moment they slid to a halt, the three saw what had Armitage so enraged; Muldoon had his M4A1 Carbine Rifle pointed at Galindo, his communication system hung from his collar and the man glared at the prisoner.

"I'm fucking telling you, boss," he said in a quiet low voice. "He's trying to lure us into a fucking trap! Why else would he suddenly be Mister Helping hands?"

Galindo didn't say a word. He just stood there with his hands in the air, looking innocent and bewildered by the sudden turn of events. Even though his face was the perfect definition of innocence, there was something about his eyes that made the newcomers wary.

"What the fuck is going on?" Carter said while his face clouded over. "Thomas! Have you lost whatever was left of your insignificant brain? Put that fucking weapon down NOW!"

Muldoon's eyes went from the drug-lord to his Captain and for an instant the man's resolve faltered. "Not gonna happen, Randy," he said after a second and his finger tightened its grip on the trigger. "This fuckwit is up to something."

Randolph Carter sighed and nodded to Nightingale. The giant lowered his weapon and circled the on-edge man; each of his steps was slow and deliberate, not making a single sound as he moved towards Muldoon.

"Why'd you say that?" the Captain asked. He held up both hands in a reassuring way, like he was dealing with a frightened stray dog.

"He's telling stories about guardians and monsters!" the sniper bellowed as his hands started trembling and sweat poured from his brow. Muldoon's complexion was pale and his eyes darted about rapidly. He looked like a crazy man.

Carter and Ward had to stop themselves from laughing. Any other time and they'd have made fun of the man. But with everything that had happened to them so far, they had to take it seriously.

"Thomas," Armitage said gently, "think about everything we've seen. Everything we've witnessed since landing. There is the possibility, right?"

Muldoon shook his head. "No. Not what he's talking about!"

"What's that?" Carter asked with a slow shake of his head. His eyes locked with Nightingale's who stood behind the shaking man, ready to grab him at a moment's notice.

Armitage sighed, then waved his hand at Galindo. The drug-lord raised an eyebrow, then understanding what the Major was saying, he spoke.

"In a time before now, long before the Conquest of Mexico, this land was full of wondrous animals and sights never seen by man. At the heart of this place, the locals erected a mighty temple. My ancestors. Inside they stored treasures, gold and riches that would've made Cortes, Pizarro or even Ponce de León drool."

Ward elbowed Carter and mumbled, "The Fountain of Youth, eh?"

"But, to guard it all," Galindo continued, and he lowered his hands, "they had to get someone to guard it. The Guardians. Terrible spirits who would do whatever they had to, to keep any and all out. Especially thieves and soldiers. We're told that the reason the valley is so full and dense is because of the blood that… fertilised the ground… is that the right word?" he asked Armitage.

Muldoon snorted back his laugh. It sounded more like a hacking cough, and the carbine rattled from the trembling. "You're a regular Wadsworth, mate."

Galindo frowned slightly at the strange name. The others caught it, and both Carter and Ward tightened their grips on their own weapons. For all his talking, the political sounding voice, his apparent care for his men and the bravado, Jorge Galindo was still a criminal and his momentary lapse in English showed that to all.

"Anyway," the Mexican said, pushing on and getting to his favourite part of the legend. "Over the ages, wars were fought and men went into the valley, trying to find the heart. Instead, all they met were death and fangs. Even the Spanish fell victim and the blood flowed so much it was like a river. That is why we don't come here. That is why my people treat this place like it's the Vatican. That is why," he stared at Muldoon and smiled, "you are all going to die here."

"Fuck that shit," Muldoon said with a growl as his finger closed around the trigger and applied pressure.

"Stand down!" Carter bellowed as his weapon snapped up while Nightingale wrapped his arms around the sniper.

Muldoon yelped and dropped his weapon the instant he felt his body raised into the air. The M4A1 clattered to the ground and roared a single shot that singed the surrounding leaves.

Galindo dropped to the ground as a branch next to his head exploded from the bullet impact. Glancing up, he saw the soldiers gathered around the two struggling men. He smiled again as his eyes went to the fallen rifle.

Carter and Armitage stood before the crazed man and stared into the wild eyes. They couldn't recognise Muldoon, all that was left behind the eyes was a man suffering and in great pain. "What's wrong with you?" Carter asked, and his voice was genuine, filled with concern.

"Doesn't matter," Armitage said sadly. "He's lost it… We can't take both him and the package with us."

"Yes, you can," Galindo said with a victorious tone to his voice.

The men turned to stare in surprise at the drug-lord holding the carbine rifle. In the struggle The Cutthroats had forgotten the fallen rifle and now, staring down the barrel held by their enemy, it was sobering.

"Told you!" Muldoon crowed. "I fucking told you so!"

"This is what's going to happen," Galindo said, and his voice was filled with power. "I'm going to walk right out of here and back to my people. My family. My life. My work. And you are all going back to the Land of Kangaroos. Empty-handed. But with the knowledge—"

His eyes went wide, and the gun slipped from his hands. The strap caught on his wrist, and it swung about. The icy touch of metal on the back of his neck froze him.

"Don't fucking move," Ward said as he reached around and removed the stray rifle. "You so much as fart and the bugs will have another snack." The medic's eyes went from the back of the man's head to the pallid complexion and sweat covered face of Muldoon and he frowned.

The struggling man's eyes were now bloodshot, and his movements were weak and useless. Each movement caused him to moan from pain and it looked as if he was about to lose control of his bodily functions.

"Boss," Ward said, "put Tommy down. Let me look at him."

The Major nodded, and Nightingale lowered the man to the ground. The moment his arms released him, Muldoon slumped to the ground and his eyes rolled back and closed.

"Tommy!" Carter shouted as he dropped to his knees over the man. "Wake up, mate!"

Ward went into action, "Sam, cover this guy. Boss, lift his head and Carter, stand the fuck back!"

CHAPTER FOURTEEN

Charles Dexter Ward's hands went all over the unconscious Muldoon's body. His keen eyes and training found nothing out of the normal. There were no obvious new wounds except for what they had sustained in the fall and river ride.

As he worked, both Nightingale and Carter kept their weapons trained on Galindo. They had rebound his hands behind his back and the drug-lord stared daggers at them.

"Keep looking, sweetheart," Carter said with a small smile. "Chuckie! What's the word?"

Not looking up from his work, the medic said, "Not the fucking bird!" His eyes went to Armitage, whose own expression was concern. "Hank, I'm gonna have to cut."

Armitage nodded while he brought out his combat knife. "Make it quick… If it's too serious, you know what to do," he said softly, and the meaning was not lost on the medic.

"It won't come to that," Ward said, taking the blade. Expertly he removed the man's combat vest then paused. "The fuck?"

Muldoon's wet shirt clung to his body, but the strange thing was the wriggling shapes that writhed about under it. Each one was thicker than a forearm, and almost as long. They tapered towards the end and from what had to be the head, blood oozed and seeped, staining the fabric.

"Get it open," Armitage ordered as Muldoon moaned and trembled again.

Ward was already doing that. Using the blade, he cut the bottom of the shirt then tore it open revealing the fat, feeding leeches. For a second the medic didn't know what to do; with normal sized ones, it would be easy. But the size of these made it almost impossible.

The team's medic grabbed the nearest leech by its tail and pulled. As he pulled up, Muldoon's skin stretched and more blood oozed from around the leech's mouth.

Ward's hand slipped slightly on the slick, pulsating insect, and the thing screeched. Letting go of it, the monster slapped against the unconscious man's chest and continued suckling.

Frowning, Ward held the knife by its handle and started working the tip under a different leech's mouth. As he wiggled the blade, more blood oozed and he could see the rows and rows of tiny sharp teeth working the flesh, sucking up more of the crimson.

"How's it going?" Carter asked, looking at the three men.

"You wanna do this?" Ward snarled as he continued trying to remove the blood-sucking creatures. It was obvious they had latched onto the man during the ride down the river. But why had it only been him? "Check yourselves," he said as he became frustrated with the lack of results.

Armitage saw the look in his man's eyes and asked, "Want me to take over?"

"No," Ward said as he used the tip to pierce the balloon-like sack of blood. The shriek from the leech made both he and Armitage flinch.

His hand spasmed from the sound, and dark red blood flowed freely from the now deflating insect. As it died, the shrieking vanished and the two men looked at one another. "That'll work," Ward said.

"We're clean," Nightingale rumbled with a sigh of relief. "Want us to check this guy?" he asked, shaking Galindo.

Armitage nodded, then frowned.

Even though they had taken out one bug, blood continued to gush from the open sack. "Can you stop it?"

"Put his head down and apply pressure," Ward ordered as he handed a thick rag to Armitage. "No matter how much blood covers your hands, do not let go. Okay?"

The Major nodded as he jammed the rag over the carcass and pressed down with as much strength as he could manage. A weak groan escaped Muldoon's lips and Armitage mumbled, "Sorry, mate. For your own good."

As Nightingale, Galindo and Carter watched on, Ward pulled out a small black and silver cylinder. He pushed a small lever, and the top flipped open, revealing a butane lighter. "This is going to fucking stink," he warned.

Pressing down on the igniter, the lighter whooshed to life as the blue flame came to life. Using his other hand, the medic turned a dial, and the flame grew higher and more intense.

"Hank," Ward said as he brought the lighter down towards the leech suckling on the skin above Muldoon's heart, "keep track of his pulse. I don't like the way his breathing looks."

Tommy Muldoon's chest rose and fell in quick movements. Each breath the man took was shallow and raspy; he didn't have much longer to live. Not if Ward had anything to do with it.

Burning flesh filled Armitage's and Ward's nose as the leech's skin was seared. It writhed, and the mouth loosened its grip ever-so, releasing a tiny fountain of blood that threatened to extinguish the lighter.

Not hesitating, the medic grabbed the bug and squeezed it tight. The head bulged as the soft innards and blood was forced up into the small opening. The medic continued to squeeze as the small mouth thrashed about, searching for a body to latch onto and feed.

"Get it over with," Armitage ordered as he grabbed the lighter. When he did, his other hand loosened its grip on the rag and fresh blood gushed from the wound. He didn't notice as he removed the other leeches feasting on Muldoon.

Ward's eyes spotted the fresh pools of blood covering the man's chest at the same time the leech he held exploded with a wet squish sound. Dropping the carcass, he said, "He's losing too much blood!"

He felt Carter's body next to him and the Captain said, "What can I do?"

"Apply as much pressure as you can. I need to sew him up. Fucking fast," Ward said as he reached into his pack and pulled out a surgical needle and thread. He held them up, then looked at Muldoon.

The unconscious man was as pale as a ghost, and the trembling was now full convulsions that shook his body hard. All three men watched as Muldoon bled out, the blood flow from the wound above his heart slowed.

Throwing the needle and thread back into his pack, Ward pulled out a tube of liquid stitches and unscrewed the cap. "Hope this fucking works," he muttered. "Randy, clean as much of the blood off as you can."

Carter nodded, then started wiping the crimson from the man's chest.

Charles Dexter Ward began pinching the openings of flesh together while squeezing the tube. Clear sticky liquid left the tip and covered the seam of the folds.

"There we go," Ward said as the blood flow eased until it stopped and the ragged breathing from Muldoon became normal.

Behind them ,Nightingale asked, "Is he gonna be okay?" He sounded like a child asking if the family dog was going to make it, and his prisoner shook his head.

Armitage looked at Ward and the medic smiled, then nodded. "He's going to make it," the Major said with a chuckle that the other three men joined until The Cutthroats were laughing loudly and Galindo looked at them, confused.

"You are a miracle worker," Carter said, patting Ward's arm. "A fucking miracle-man!"

Ward shook his head as he felt for Muldoon's pulse. "Fuck off with that shit. I'm just good at my job—"

One of the closed wounds reopened with a tear and eruption of dark red blood that splattered the three men's face. "Fucking hell!" Carter said as he spat, trying to rid himself of the iron substance.

"No!" Ward said as he struggled to keep the soldier from bleeding out. His hands moved fast, applying more of the glue-like substance to the now re-opened wounds.

"What the fuck is that?" Nightingale asked. His eyes focused on the large, brown, hairy thing emerging from the ground behind Armitage.

Jorge Galindo's body shook from fear and his hand instinctively gripped the giant's sleeve. "Jesús, me levantaré. Jesús, acompáñame. Jesús, encierra mi corazón en el tuyo y deja que mi cuerpo y mi alma te sean encomendados. El Señor está crucificado. Que Dios guarde y proteja mis sentidos para que las desgracias no me superen. En el nombre de Dios, el Padre, el Hijo y el Espíritu Santo. Amén," the man mumbled as he tried to back away.

Nightingale felt the man's body press into him and his training took over. "Steady there," he whispered as his eyes darted about, taking in the ground properly.

Surrounding the five men were ten meter round flat discoloured 'lids'. Each one was made from a mixture of materials; branches, leaves and pieces of moss that were packed down on top of the burrows.

"Boss," Nightingale said as he recognised the homes of Trap-door Spiders, "we've got company. On your six."

CHAPTER FIFTEEN

Before Henry Armitage could react, his body was heaved into the air by the long front legs of the spider. He screamed and felt his body being crushed by the massive arachnid's strength.

"Fucking hell!" Carter said as he and Ward rolled away from the struggling duo.

They brought their weapons up, ready to open fire, but the way the spider was thrashing about fighting against Armitage's own considerable strength made it difficult to get a clean shot.

"Shoot this fucking thing!" the Major ordered as he gasped for air. Armitage could tell his ribs were cracking and that soon they would break, splintering until they pierced his lungs and heart. "Fucking kill it!"

The four men watched as the monster began to retreat into its burrow. They knew that the moment it passed the threshold and closed the lid, the team leader was dead.

Carter took action. He pulled the pin from a grenade and tossed it into the opening behind the spider. "Chuckie," he said as they waited for the explosion, "keep Tommy alive. Got it?"

Before the medic could answer, the ground behind the spider and man roared and shook from the detonation.

The lid was incinerated by the force and dark plumes of

smoke billowed into the air as debris rained down on the men. Carter threw himself across the body and shielded Muldoon from any larger chunks.

Stopping its retreat, the spider turned to see its home destroyed. From out of the fiery hole, man-sized versions of it crawled out, whimpering and on fire. They were its young, and it watched, helpless, as they burned to death and collapsed into a rotting, stinking heap.

"Estás jodido," Galindo said as the massive body shook with rage.

Turning, the eight eyes spotted Carter who was rolling on the ground, trying to put himself out. The Captain felt the gaze then spun. His rifle screamed as he pulled the trigger.

A shriek of pain and anger came from the spider as the tiny bullets riddled its body. Minute explosions dotted the thorax and legs, letting blood flow.

"Aim… for… the… head!" Armitage gasped each word as darkness crept around the edge of his vision.

"How's Tommy?" Carter asked as he peered through the scope, trying to get a bead on the face.

Ward shook his head, "Not fucking good. That explosion reopened the rest of his wounds and gave him some new ones… I need help!"

"On it!" Nightingale bellowed as he bounded over to his brothers, his own carbine firing at the spider.

Each wave of attack pushed the spider back, but its powerful front legs squeezed ever tighter and tighter. Its prey gasped and screamed as the life was pushed from its body and the moment the man was dead, it would feast.

"Oh, fuck me," Nightingale said as he got a proper look at the monster. The long fangs dripped with venom and the eyes were covered in crust and dried blood. "Think I'm gonna be sick." Holding back his disgust at the sight of the spider's face, the giant dropped to his knees.

"Monitor his pulse and breathing," Ward ordered as he used the needle and thread to sew up the wounds. There wasn't much blood seeping from the holes, and that worried him even more. "Don't you fucking die!"

"I can't feel a strong pulse," Nightingale said before he looked up at the spider.

Randolph Carter charged towards the spider, his carbine spewing bullets at the arachnid. As he fired, his eyes were glued to the now still body of Armitage. The Captain couldn't tell if his friend was dead, alive, or just knocked out. It didn't matter though. What did was getting everyone home safely. Including Galindo.

The weapon clicked empty. Instead of loading a fresh clip the soldier pulled out his combat knife.

Screaming like a banshee, Carter raised the blade as he ran full speed under the spider. The war cry caught the attention of the arachnid, but it couldn't see the attacking man.

A momentary burning sensation washed over its stomach and then the bite of cold steel was followed by warm and wet splattering the ground and its legs.

The spider wobbled as blood oozed and dribbled from the long ugly gash along its underside. After a second the beast steadied itself and turned, dropping Armitage as it focused all its attention on Carter, whose smile of triumph was replaced with an 'oh shit' look.

Armitage's body rolled, and the man gasped, coughed, then groaned. His eyes fluttered open, and he barked, "Regroup! Keep that thing away from Tommy!"

Turning his head, the one-eyed man saw Ward frantically trying to stop Muldoon's wounds reopening yet again and to cease the constant flow of blood. The eye went to the patient's face and the mixture of sweat and the deathly pale tone did not give him any confidence. "Chuck," he said as the pounding of Carter's feet and the roar of his rifle filled the air. "Chuck, is he gonna make it?"

"Keep that thing off us and maybe!"

Henry Armitage nodded. There was something wrong with the situation, but he couldn't tell what. It felt like this was only the beginning. "Sammy," his voice sounded strange to his ears, foreign and raspy, "look around and tell me what's wrong."

Muscles moving on their own, the leader of The Cutthroats brought his carbine up and fired. Behind him he could hear the grunts and mutterings of the team's medic and the rapid footsteps of the giant.

The bullets did the job, and the spider became licked in position. The front legs were up and in front of the face, shielding it. The long thick hairs provided ample cover, acting like armour and most of the bullets seemed to vanish without doing much damage. Its back six legs shuffled, moving the bulk back and forth in a strange dance.

"Can't keep this up much longer," Carter said as he slammed a fresh clip into his M4A1.

Armitage couldn't help himself and said, "That's what she said!"

"Really?" Nightingale said as he joined the men, his rifle adding its voice to the choir of destruction. He stood right in front of Ward and Muldoon, his body blocking them completely and smiled, "How we looking?"

"Almost out and getting well and truly shitted off with this shit!" Carter said in a tone reserved for a comedy routine.

Nightingale laughed. "Join the club," he said. "It's clear as far as I can tell. But we need to keep moving."

He was right, and they knew it. The longer they remained still, making as much noise as they were, eventually they'd attract something bigger and more dangerous. Unfortunately, they couldn't do anything until they had seen to Muldoon.

"Oi! You want to set up the blanket for the picnic, or would you rather do your fucking job and put this cunt down?" Carter's voice cracked like a whip, snapping Nightingale out of his stupor. "Fucking shoot!"

"Sir!" the giant barked without realising. His finger hit the trigger and the rifle fired.

Armitage's one good eye studied the rapid, staccato movements of the arachnid and a feeling of dread settled in his stomach. *At this rate,* he thought, *we'll run out of ammo before doing any actual damage.* He had to act, not only to save Muldoon, but all of them.

"Fire in the hole!" he cried as the last of his grenades left his hand.

It landed with barely a sound to the right of the spider who didn't register its existence.

The three men; Carter, Nightingale and Armitage, dropped to the soft ground a second before the explosion.

A cloud of dust, debris and flame rocked the arachnid, but it didn't fall. The legs kept it upright and stable. But its movements were slower, more careful and measured. It was like the monster was now even more wary of its prey.

"Fuck me!" Armitage groaned as he watched the spider spin and raise its abdomen.

The men heard a groan followed by a grunt as the spider shot a line of thicker than bone web at them, the end of which expanded to resemble a grasping hand.

Randolph Carter dove, his arms wrapping around the startled Ward. The two rolled out of the way just as a strand of the sticky line latched onto the unconscious man's blood-stained chest.

"Now!" the Major shouted. He didn't focus on Muldoon's body being dragged towards an ugly death. All he saw was the unprotected arse.

Bullets tore the flesh, and the spider howled in pain. Spinning, its front legs grabbed the web and increased the speed at which it pulled the meal towards itself. The fangs dribbled a noxious mixture of venom and saliva that sizzled the moment it touched the ground.

"For fuck's sake!" Armitage said as he quickly reloaded. He didn't understand why his men weren't following orders. "Now's our chance!"

Next to him, the one-eyed man heard Ward mutter, "See you soon, Tommy."

Risking a look, the team leader saw his remaining men watch the spider wrap their fallen brother in more web, like a mother swaddling its baby. Their faces were ashen, filled with sadness and anguish at the rapid loss of their own. They stared as the spider raised the cocoon to its mouth and the fangs came down, piercing the flesh with a fountain of blood erupting from the punctures.

Within seconds, they knew that Tommy Muldoon was dead.

At the sight of another man killed in action, something inside of Henry Armitage snapped. His face set in stone, the man raised his M4A1 and stared into the scope.

Even though Muldoon's body was encased in the thick web,

the bulge of the grenades attached to his belt was noticeable.

Taking a breath, Armitage's finger closed around the trigger and he applied the correct amount of pressure. He felt the shot crack, then the rifle kick and his chest ached.

The single round sped through the air until it found the egg-shaped explosive.

The sudden mixture of the gunpowder and the liquid webbing inside the arachnid vaporised as a roar filled the air at the same time. The massive ball of liquid fire devastated the area, burning everything it touched and spreading like napalm.

Everything but two of the spider's legs remained. The rest was nothing but fire and an enormous crater.

The four remaining members of The Cutthroats blinked and shook their heads. All felt as if a flash-bang grenade had gone off next to them and they knew that later on they'd have the same feeling as a nasty hangover. Only this time take-away food wouldn't help it.

"Report!" Armitage wheezed as he slowly got to his feet. Every part of him ached, and he looked around, amazed at how fast the jungle burned.

Next to him Carter coughed then laughed. "That worked a fucking treat!" he smiled at the sight of the other trap doors burning. The smell of cooked meat filled the air and his smile grew bigger. "Why didn't we do that earlier?"

"Never mind," his friend said while helping Ward to his feet. "You okay?"

The medic nodded, then sniffed back tears. "Fuck, this shit burns. We better get out of here ASAP."

Henry Armitage nodded, then turned to the communications officer. "Grab Galindo and we'll move out."

The giant looked like a child who fucked up. "Sorry, boss," he said as he raised his hands in apology. "But the fuckwit's gone."

CHAPTER SIXTEEN

Jorge Galindo laughed as he used a collection of vines to pull himself up. The fall and roll down the muddy slope knocked the wind out of him, and he took the time to right himself as a breather.

While he caught his breath, the man smiled; large and bordering on the hysterical, Galindo couldn't believe his luck. He'd finally escaped from the soldiers, and hopefully they were already dead. *Si no lo son,* he thought, looking at his surroundings, *pronto lo serán.*

The way the trees bent and curled around each other, creating a tunnel of shadows and green, looked familiar to him and Galindo continued to smile.

From deep within him, he felt a joyous howl of laughter rise, and even though the drug-lord had a good idea where he was, he couldn't risk attracting the attention of more bichos. All he had to do was make it to the safe house, contact his friends and start all over again.

It would be a long struggle, hell maybe even impossible. Then again, he deserved a rest. Maybe, as he rebuilt everything, he'd disappear with his family for a while. Go travelling and see the other side.

But, of course, the moment his men started resurrecting the compound, recruiting more sicarios farmers and the women he'd need to be on-site to keep everyone under control. "No hay descanso para los malvados," he muttered, then cackled.

He took a step forward, and instantly he knew where he was. It wouldn't take too long for him to reach safety, and from there even less time out of the Valley.

Si esos imbéciles siguen vivos, he thought as he started off into the tropical jungle, *te prometo abuela, que sufrirán hasta el último aliento*. He figured it'd take an hour at most to reach his safe house, if it was still standing. It was years since he'd last been there, and only the Gods knew if it still stood.

Jorge Galindo continued his trek forward, the promise of rising again like a phoenix propelling him. There was nothing standing before him, nothing or nobody that could stop his grim purpose. And if any got in his way, they'd meet the same fate as those pendejo soldiers from the land of kangaroos.

The jungle seemed to part as the hysterically laughing man danced through the foliage; skipping over the large gnarled roots, swinging from vines and low-hanging branches, and all the while laughing and planning his glorious return.

A single thought ran through his head, a mission statement that would become his mantra and the mantra of the new and improved cartel. He would scream it from the highest peaks so the world would know his power and voice.

This time round, Jorge Galindo would be unstoppable. His will, stronger than iron, harder than steel with the ability to bend men to his will and never falter in his goals.

As he continued making his way through the Lacandon Jungle, mind focused on the future and all his plans, the drug-lord didn't see the pit. Nor did he feel his foot step on empty air, and by the time he realised that he was falling, it was too late.

Galindo screamed as the wet mud and earth embraced him. His face submerged under the dirt; the man's mind went into survival mode but without the use of his senses, panic set in. A deep breath resulted in the filth filling his lungs and threatening to suffocate him. He couldn't breathe and struggled to get himself free.

His legs flailed about, kicking wildly at the air as his arms dug in and pushed with all their might. The mud and dirt surrounded Galindo, closing further around him, and each time he cleared some of it away, the rush of air sucked him deeper into it.

The drug-lord felt his lungs ache as they begged for air, but he couldn't breathe. To do so would be death and there was no way in hell he, Jorge Galindo, would die in the middle of the fucking Lacandon Jungle. His destiny was to unite Mexico and live until he died old and in the bosom of a senorita.

Unable to see with barely the capability to hear or even cry out for help, Jorge Galindo's mind raced. He'd seen men and some children drown and suffocate in similar ways, and he knew there wasn't anything to do except give in and die. Or. Find a way out of the situation.

Which, if he was honest with himself, wasn't the worst he'd been in.

All he had to do, the only thing of importance for him, was to get his nose clear of the mud and breathe. Once that was done and he wasn't at risk of choking on the horrid mixture of dirt and water, he'd be able to put his full attention to getting the rest of himself free.

Which was easier said than done. Every single muscle in his body was tense, ready to leap into action and cause more problems. The man directed his willpower towards forcing the muscles to relax, which allowed him to pull from the reservoir of strength he somehow always pulled from and work on lifting his head up.

The layers of dirt, water and mud that covered his entire body were already drying from the rays of sunlight hitting his back and the humidity. It felt like he was covered in a hard shell that weighed more than the last woman he ever paid for. But what made him panic, shiver and push harder were the worms slithering through the layers around his head and neck. Each of the slimy invertebrates slid their wet bodies across his flesh, and the man wanted to scream and run back to the safety of his compound.

After straining for a few seconds, Galindo came to the realisation that there was no way he'd be able to lift his head straight up. His mind conjured up the image of the last man he'd forced to wander into one of the few quick sand pools in the jungle. Even after the Narco's head was under, the screams were still audible until the last breath and the death rattle bubbled up.

But there was always a way out. He'd learned that from the old boss, and all he had to do was calm himself enough to figure it out.

Through the mud that had settled into his ear canals, Galindo heard a scratching sound. It reminded him of the way a dog's claws sounded when digging a hole, and his mind went through all the known tribes in the area.

It grew in volume, which meant only one thing. Whatever was digging through the ground was getting closer!

Turning his head to focus on the approaching sound, Galindo felt the hardened shell crack and slowly crumble. The shards tumbled from his back and the sudden rush of air that filled his lungs and mouth sent a shiver of joy through him.

With each shake of his head, more and more of the mud fell from his body. But there was a problem, a tightness surrounding his body that did not come from the mud.

A final vicious shake of his head freed it and with an almighty gasp, Jorge Galindo could breathe again.

His relief was temporarily lived for as soon as he gasped and laughed at his luck, the tightness around his body increased, and the pressure forced the air from his lungs with a yelp of pain.

A moment later the world tilted as Galindo was lifted from the ground and shook violently. His teeth rattled as the rest of the dried shell of mud shattered, then fell to the pit's floor. When he felt the pressure from his face leave, the man opened his eyes and immediately regretted doing so.

Covering his body from the shoulders down were human-sized claws that dug into his flesh and continued to apply pressure. Following them, Galindo's eyes saw the head-sized brown and black segments of the eight meter long centipede.

His mind raced as he recognised the markings of it. He'd seen it before, in Sonora, and the name flashed through his mind; Scolopendra heros or the giant Sonoran centipede and that name sent another shiver down his spine and the warmth of piss leaving his bladder.

Si salgo de esto, he thought as he struggled to find a way out of the bug's grasp, *prometo salvar a tantas mujeres de los prostíbulos como pueda.*

Lifting his head, the drug-lord's eyes stared into the pitch black, soulless, segmented eyes of the centipede. Looking into nothing but emptiness reminded the man of a shark's eyes, and a part of Galindo knew he was a dead man.

There was no way he could talk his way out of this. No amount of money would pay for his freedom, and that realisation was shattering.

A vile smell filled his nostrils, and Galindo finally saw the rotting carcasses that littered the pit's floor and walls. All were animals, not other insects, but the local wildlife; spider monkeys, red macaws, tapirs, a jaguar and a couple of howler monkeys. Each one was in a different state of decay, but he knew the way the centipede fed and his mind conjured the image of his own decomposing body adding to the stench.

A click caught his attention and Galindo's eyes darted to the brightly coloured serrated mandibles. They moved slowly, opening and closing with a strange rhythm that was hypnotic.

Bright white liquid oozed from the tips and dropped to the floor with a sizzling sound. It was the bug's venom and the moment it touched his skin, Galindo was dead.

The man grunted as he fell to the ground. Landing on skeletal remains of a howler monkey, Galindo rolled, then gasped.

Another centipede was wrapped around the first one, locked in a battle of wills, and the prize was a fresh meal. Watching in awe, they reminded Jorge Galindo of a moment from his childhood when he watched two snakes fight over a lizard. The way they moved was the same as the centipedes, although these bugs used their hands to tear pieces of exoskeleton away.

As the insects continued to struggle, they fell and rolled about. The rapid movements, the thrashing about, kicked up mud and pieces of flesh and bone.

Galindo scrambled out of the way until his back was jammed against one of the pit's walls. He tried to disappear, hoping that the fighting centipedes would forget him. The man's hands reached out, searching for anything he could use as a weapon. Just in case.

Something rough, long and reminiscent of bone filled his hand and Galindo pulled it up. The bone rattled as it followed its new trajectory. The rest of the skeleton, the man couldn't tell what it was, loudly sang as it broke and fell.

"Ya valí madre," Jorge Galindo said to himself as the centipedes stopped and as one turned their heads towards the man. Their antennae twitched at the sound of his voice, the black eyes stared into his soul and the drug-lord uttered a prayer before bringing the bones up as protection.

CHAPTER SEVENTEEN

"Hello there!" Carter's voice sounded friendly, but the edge to it betrayed that fact. "Need a hand, do we?"

Galindo looked up and fought the smile that spread across his face. Even though he was happy to see the four soldiers peering down at him, they'd do what they could to rescue him, a part of the drug-lord had hoped they were dead and being eaten by the spiders.

"Say the magic word," the giant rumbled and the deep voice caught the attention of the centipedes.

The two bugs slowly untangled one from the other and they reared up onto their back legs as the twin sets of antennae swivelled about, studying the newcomers. The rows of claws reached out, making tiny grasping motions towards the men standing above them. Whatever they smelled from these men, the centipedes wanted a piece.

"What's the magic word?" Nightingale asked with a cheeky grin. Although he smiled, his eyes were dead and had the look of being ready to choke the Mexican. "Say it!"

Below him, the centipedes climbed up the dirt and root covered wall. Their claws dug in and the insects easily scurried up towards their meal.

Galindo's eyes watched, and he smiled. It would only take one of them to get him out of the pit, and even then, it'd be a simple task to either overpower or convince the men to be his new bodyguard. Desperate men were always easier to deal with. Looking at the two men, it was obvious they were running on fumes and could easily be turned to his own purpose.

"Don't think he wants to be saved," Carter said as he raised his rifle. His finger squeezed the trigger twice and one bug froze.

Two bullet holes allowed blood and bright pink matter to ooze from out its eyes. The antenna twitched and spasmed as the insect's nervous system shutdown. Its mandibles clicked open, shut, then opened one last time before the claws released their grasp and the lifeless husk fell.

Across the pit, Ward and Armitage stood. The team medic had his M4A1 up and aimed at the other centipede who was getting closer and closer to Carter's boots.

"Jorge," Armitage's voice sounded as if it came from deep within a well, "look at me."

Galindo flinched at the sound of his name, and a section of mud next to his head exploded as another massive centipede appeared from within the earth. Its mandibles clacked loudly as it waved its head back and forth, trying to latch onto the flesh it so desired.

Without hesitation, Henry Armitage's carbine bellowed and the head of the latest addition emptied in a fountain of blood and juices. The pungent cocktail splattered Galindo's face, and the horrid flavour assaulting his mouth made him retch.

"Get over here, right fucking now!" the one-eyed man ordered while Carter, Ward and Nightingale fired at the remaining bug.

The bullets tore through the exoskeleton like it was tissue paper. With each bullet hit, the centipede cried out in pain. An alien sound unlike anything the men had ever heard before. It reminded them of an animal begging for death after being hit by a car, and each cry of agony froze the five men.

The Cutthroats' fingers remained on the triggers of their M4A1s, shredding the insect's body until it was nothing more than a bloody, pulpy mess.

"Think that'll fucking do, mates," Carter said as one by one their weapons clicked empty. The Captain let the empty clip drop to the ground, but he didn't reload yet. Instead, he stared at the blood-splattered man cowering among the corpses and bones. "I'm not fucking fishing him out."

Both Ward and Nightingale nodded in agreement with the man, then they turned away and reloaded their weapons. Neither man could look at the drug-lord, all they could do was focus on making it back home and mourn the loss of their brothers. Until that happened, though, all they could do was the absolute bare minimum in keeping their prisoner alive.

Armitage glanced at the three men who were taking the moment to have a break. He understood well enough their lack of enthusiasm for rescuing Galindo, but there was no way he'd let them fail the mission. Not after the cataclysmic loss they'd suffered.

Bending down, the Major extended his hand. "Time to go," he said in the same tone of voice used when calling a frightened animal.

The Mexican didn't move. He cowered, hiding his face behind his hands, and shivered.

"Galindo!" Armitage snapped, and the man flinched. "It's over," he said gently. "Take my fucking hand"

A small smile formed slowly across Galindo's face as he understood the soldier. He ran across the pit, then leaped the moment he made it to the wall.

Using all the strength he had left, Henry Armitage pulled while Jorge Galindo kicked at the wall. The drug-lord's boots pushed the loose earth away, creating cavities that made it more difficult for him to get a purchase and climb.

"Need a fucking hand," Armitage growled as his left shoulder screamed with pain. With the weight of the struggling Galindo, it felt as if his shoulder would dislocate at any second. His right hand reached down and grabbed the Mexican, helping with the effort. "Help!"

Carter appeared next to him saying, "Hold ya fucking horses." His calloused hands reached down and gripped Galindo's wrists. "On three."

"Three!" Armitage shouted without counting, and the two men

pulled the drug-lord up easily.

The moment he passed the threshold, the three men rolled, coughed, and Galindo laughed. It began as a low chuckle that grew to a loud, almost hysterical bellow.

Armitage and Carter exchanged confused looks at the sight of the criminal mastermind rolling on the ground, laughing like a clown, while kicking his legs into the air.

The major scrambled to his feet, then grabbed the laughing man.

¡Muchas gracias, amigo mío!" Galindo gushed while giving Armitage a bear hug. "Los dioses te sonríen—"

He grunted, then stumbled from the punch. Rubbing his jaw, Galindo tasted blood from the fresh cut on his lip. Eyes flashed, he spun, growling, ready to fight back. "¡¿Quién demonios te crees que eres, güey?!" the man snarled.

Armitage's fist flew again and landed with a heavy thud. He felt Galindo's body contort and wrap around his hand, trembling from the gut punch. With his other hand, the team leader reached around, grabbed Galindo by the back of his head and whispered, "I'm the man who is going to keep you alive but you try any shit like that again, I'll let my men have you."

With a grunt of discomfort, Galindo spun so he could see the other three men. Each stared at him with the same level of compassion one has for a rat. Carter held up his knife and said, "The knife or my gun?"

Both shoulders ached from the sudden wrenching they felt as both his arms were pulled behind his back. Armitage slipped another set of cable-tie handcuffs around his wrists and said, "Now play nice and maybe you'll get a lemon slice at the end."

Nightingale held up his hand to silence the others. His face was drawn into an expression of pure concentration as he listened to the radio headset. After a second, he nodded and picked up the microphone. "Roger that, Zero Two Four. We'll be there with bells on. But, be advised there is a possibility of it being a hot zone. Make sure you've got plenty of heavy artillery with you. Over."

"ETA?" Carter said as he reloaded his carbine before sliding the clip out of his Kimber and counting the rounds.

"Ten minutes max," Nightingale said as he followed Carter

and checked his ammo and weapons. “Fuck, I’m low.”

Ward did the same and nodded, “We all are. Hope there isn’t anything waiting for us.”

“Just a pinche fire,” Galindo said with a gesture of his head that made the men look.

Behind them, the fire raged on, consuming everything in its path. Huge black clouds billowed high into the air, and in the distance the five men could barely see the reflection from the helicopter’s blade.

“Move out,” Armitage said, and there was a tinge of hope mixed with panic to his voice. “We need to get to the EVAC zone and set up a perimeter before they do.”

CHAPTER EIGHTEEN

"Is this the place?" Carter said as he wiped sweat from his bald head. He was red and had trouble breathing from the intense pace his friend had set. "Please fucking tell me this is the fucking cunt place!"

Armitage turned to Nightingale. "What were the coordinates?"

The giant cleared his throat, took a long sip from his canteen then said, "Right here, boss. Stake my pay on it."

"You're staking all our lives," Carter said with a shake of his head. Turning, he saw the glow of the flames approaching. "Right, listen up wankers," he said and his voice got the attention of the four other men. "I want a tight perimeter. Nothing gets in, got it? Everyone does their job and listens to the others." He pointed to the approaching forest fire and continued, "We are not going to be here by the time that arrives. Understand me?"

Nightingale nodded, then stopped. His eyes went wide, and he lifted a trembling hand. "Randy," he said, "behind you."

Turning slowly, Randolph Carter saw the twin sedan-sized pincers appear from the trees. They clacked open and shut as the long, bigger than a tank body of a scorpion emerged. Its tail was raised straight up with the tip curving down, ready to strike. A white liquid bubbled, then dripped from the tip of the stinger and the five men stepped back without thinking.

"Figures," Armitage said as he raised his M4A1. He wasn't surprised to see the scorpion hungrily snapping its pincers open and closed. In fact, it was the cherry on top of the fucked-up sundae that was the mission.

They watched as the tail whipped to the side, clearing the tops of trees without a problem. A jaguar screamed as it fell from the branch it was perched upon.

One pincer snapped out and grabbed the animal from the air. It scratched, hissed and snarled, trying to look intimidating. It winced in pain and whimpered as the serrated edges of the pincer closed, slicing the enormous cat's flesh, letting blood seep from the wound and stain the ground.

The pincer then fed the torso into the small, mandible covered mouth. It slobbered and drooled the meal down, then cleaned itself.

"Do we have enough ammo?" Armitage asked as his mind tried to remember any weaknesses a scorpion had.

Ward shook his head as he took a step backwards. "Not fucking likely," he said. "That thing looks like a goddamn tank!"

Armitage nodded. The medic was right, but he didn't like the chance of running. There was something about the way the scorpion's legs moved in anticipation that worried him. "Ammo check. Right fucking now," he said as his hand quickly counted how many grenades he had left. None.

"Fucking fucked," Carter said as he held up three full clips. "I've got maybe less than half in the Kimber and even fewer grenades."

Ward laughed, his voice cracking as the sight of the pincers opening and closing slowly terrified him. "Can I just say, whatever the plan is, it's fucking crazy!"

"Like nothing else you've done so far?" Nightingale said. His hand dove into his pack and pulled out four blocks of plastic explosives. A smile broke out across his face and he showed Armitage, "Someone up there loves me!"

"We get through this and I'll love you long time," Carter said, beating his friend to the punch. "But, first thing's first. What's the game plan?"

Henry Armitage kept his eye on the scorpion. Studying the segments, he looked for any signs of a weak spot. “Easy,” he said, finally looking at the blocks of C4, “we kill the fucking cunt. And any others that come our way. Questions?”

Before Ward could speak, Sam Nightingale raised his hand. “I’ve got a couple,” he said in a small voice.

“How the fuck are we supposed to kill THAT?” Ward bellowed while pointing at the monstrosity. His eyes were wild with fright.

“Oh, that’s better than mine,” the giant said as he lowered his hand. It wrapped around the plastic and cradled them gently, almost like they were a baby he didn’t want to wake up.

“Thanks,” Ward said, then looked at his superiors with an expectant look.

Behind the men, the scorpion took a step forward and clacked its pincers loudly. The sound bounced off the trees and the echo shook the highest, weakest branches of the canopy. Its segmented body bunched together, and the tail curled menacingly and swayed like a cat ready to pounce.

“Shit, that thing looks fierce,” Carter said, noticing the bright white poison dripping from the tip of the stinger. “Hope this isn’t going to be an epic boss fight.”

“Killjoy,” Armitage said with a devil may care smile. He adjusted the straps around his shoulder and hefted the carbine. It was banged up, covered in scratches with the scope and silencer long forgotten. “It’s simple,” he said, using his most controlled and awe-inspiring voice. “Charles, you and Randy will get that thing’s attention and keep it. Lure it down towards us, do whatever you have to. But keep it focused on you,” he looked to Nightingale. “See those trees there?”

The giant nodded and smiled. “Just like in Germany. Right?”

At the sound of the country’s name, the two other men gasped. They were too busy focusing on the scorpion and not shitting their pants that they didn’t think of any strategies.

“You sure it’ll work?” Carter asked while looking at the trees. “They don’t look heavy enough.”

“Probably,” Armitage agreed as he watched the scorpion grab a cricket carcass and started its meal. The tail still swayed in its hypnotic way, while the beady eyes watched the men. *That's the dangerous part*, he thought as he continued speaking. "But all we need to do is trap it. Just long enough to take down that thing's tail."

"Why the fuck is the tail important?" Ward asked, genuinely surprised. "Isn't it better to go for the head?"

Carter shook his head as he readied himself for the coming battle. "The tail is the weakest point. And with how low our ammo supplies are, it makes perfect sense."

"Exactly," Armitage said as he watched Nightingale run over to the trees. "Leave one for me!" he shouted before looking at the others. "You've got your orders. If you run out of bullets, use the grenades. When that well dries, run as fast as you can."

Carter and Ward said nothing. They nodded, turned, then as one jogged towards the slobbering armour-covered bug.

Charles Dexter Ward looked at his Captain. Carter's face was blank, as if he was mentally preparing himself for death. That thought sent a shiver up and down his spine, and the medic yanked back on the M4A1's slide. The metallic clink of the first round sliding into the chamber made him smile. "How do you want to do this?"

"No reason to be subtle," Carter said as he raised his own weapon. His voice was hollow, the same as his eyes, and he walked with a singular purpose; to kill the creature, or die trying.

Ward nodded, "Makes sense." Bringing the rifle up to his shoulder, the man stared down the sight and barrel. The scorpion stood motionless. Even the excited movement of its legs had ceased. Now, the only movement from the animal was the gentle back and forth of the stinger.

Carter's finger closed around the trigger, and he exhaled before squeezing it.

The scorpion reared back as the hail of bullets bounced off its hard exoskeleton. Barely a scratch was left, and the bug growled, low and guttural, the sound was like the engine of an actual tank gearing up.

"Think that made it angry," Ward said before he too fired. His face was illuminated by flashes as the gunpowder was lit and exploded.

An ugly pincer came up and covered the eyes of the scorpion. With a groan, the monster lurched forward, the legs pulling hard against the suction of the wet earth. Its tail rose high, ready to plunge into the body of the puny treats attacking it.

"Reloading," Carter said as he let the empty clip sink to the ground. Next to him, Ward continued to fire in short controlled bursts. It amazed Carter at how well the medic grouped his shots. It was like he wanted to piss off the tank-sized scorpion.

Gradually the two men moved backwards, each step placed with all the care the situation allowed them. They had to be careful as any misstep would cause a fall then death by pincers and mandibles. Neither man wanted to experience the sensation of having their chest punctured then feeling the same sensation of a serrated knife slicing into soft, spongy flesh.

"Wonder how Hank and Sammy are doing?" Carter said as he began a second round of firing. It was a genuine question, but also a way to keep Ward's attention.

The medic tried looking back, but his neck wouldn't twist that far. "No clue," he said as they continued backpedalling. The scorpion's speed hadn't changed as it continued approaching the men. A pincer was raised still, protecting its face, and the other swiped at them with little effort. It seemed as if it was playing with them, just like a cat.

"We're set here," Armitage's voice was a whisper in their ears. "You two look like you're having fun. Want to bring the party to us?"

"Oh," the other man said with a chuckle as the scorpion slipped on the jaguar's blood and mud. It toppled with a grunt. "We should be able to manage that."

Above them, they could hear the telltale mechanical roar of rotor blades slicing through the air and the groan of metal twisting against the air. Carter tilted his head and listened while the scorpion tried to get back up. "That's a Black Hawk!" he said happily.

Ward followed suit, tilting his head to listen and a massive smile spread across his face. Tears welled up, and the medic wanted to cry there and then.

"Eyes on the prize, boys."

Hearing the Major's voice made Carter and Ward spin. They dove backwards, narrowly avoiding the pincer swipe. The two rolled as they felt the earth shake with the quick movements of the gigantic insect.

The stinger came down and pierced the wet earth in rapid succession, kicking up the ground and pieces of dead cricket. Each strike was with more anger and the scorpion's mandibles worked overtime. Obviously it had never worked this hard for its meal.

"You've got him good and pissed," Armitage said as he studied the bug. "Get it further down, another couple of meters. Then, give it all you got. Once it's nice and furious, throw your grenades then run for your life… We'll take care of the rest."

Ward hefted the grenade he held. "Got a better idea," he said before using his thumb to pull the pin.

Carter blinked, "What the fuck are you doing?"

A small grunt came from the medic as he over-extended his arm. The throw was good, but overshot the front of the monster. It bounced along the hard shell and landed with a wet thud behind it.

"Chuck!" Armitage said. "What the fuck?"

Ignoring his commanding officer, the medic raised his gun and fired. His eye caught Carter in his peripheral and said, "Little help here."

Without thinking, the Captain joined in. His carbine roared as he emptied the clip.

The bullets bounced off the exoskeleton, but the creature's momentum had ceased. Even though there was no chance of the bullets doing any serious damage, the scorpion's instinct to protect itself took over.

Armitage, Carter and Nightingale watched, trying to figure out when the grenade would detonate. There was nothing they could do except wait and watch. The mounting tension became unbearable and Armitage couldn't take it anymore. "If he wastes a grenade," he growled. "I'll tear out his intestines myself."

"Calm your tits, boss," Charles Dexter Ward said while making a calming gesture with his free hand. "When it goes, get the fuck out of the way," he said to the man next to him.

The second-in-command nodded and shifted the weight on his feet. His mind ran through the most likely outcomes. Nearly all ended in the same way; both of them dead and in the belly of a giant scorpion. "Love this plan," he said, loading a fresh clip into the gun. "You are truly a master tactician."

"Blow it out your hole," Ward said as they fought to keep the scorpion at bay. "It'll work," he said, gritting his teeth.

As the other man opened his mouth to make yet another comment, the ground behind the monster erupted in an explosion of dirt, mud and fragments of cricket. The ball bearings tore into the ass of the scorpion in an eruption of bright red blood and tiny shards of black shell.

The tail dipped slightly, then pushed forward as the force of the explosion threatened to flip the creature. Its pincers flailed wildly and the tiny eyes blinked in panic.

Carter and Ward turned, then ran at full speed towards Armitage and Nightingale. Behind them, the scorpion had righted itself and was charging at the men. Its legs propelled it forward at such a speed it surprised all watching.

"Dive to the side!" Armitage shouted. "Sam, you ready?"

The giant nodded, then gave a big thumbs up as he held up the detonator.

Ward and Carter jumped, diving into the bushes as the scorpion couldn't stop its trajectory. The pincers dug into the soft earth, trying to stop itself as the legs backpedalled like crazy.

Nightingale squinted; he had to time it just right and the moment he spotted the pincer crossing his imaginary line. the man depressed the trigger.

Six large trees shook as it vaporised their trunks in a halo of smoke and fire. With a look of curiosity, the enormous bug turned and looked up at the now trembling trees. Slowly, they swayed, then fell with a loud creak.

The remnants of The Cutthroats watched as the now dead trees fell, crushing the scorpion under their weight. The mud helped to suck it down, and the air was filled with a high-pitched. pig-like squeal. Its tail curled up, ready to strike anything and everything.

The men watched as Henry Armitage quickly scrambled up the shiny slick shell protecting the soft squishy insides. He wiped sweat from his brow and stared into the monster's eyes.

"You afraid, ain't ya?" he said with a smile. The eyes looked up at him and the expression could only be called fright. It made Armitage laugh like a maniac and without hesitation he pulled out his Kimber and unloaded the clip right into its face.

The bullets ripped and tore through the ocular organs. Armitage continued laughing as blood and white slimy goo covered him.

His gun clicked empty. The soldier's next move was to pull out the block of C4 he carried and attach it to the disfigured, mangled face. "Blow it!" he bellowed, leaping from the arachnid.

CHAPTER NINETEEN

"I still can't believe that actually worked!" Carter said as he clambered over a fallen tree. His M4A1 clanged against the wood, then smacked his leg. He winced; the hit would cause a large bruise on his thigh. *That's going to hurt in the morning*, he thought.

Ward laughed, though it sounded more like a cackle. "Honestly? You and me both, mate," he said as he lumbered over the log.

"Quiet back there," Armitage said as he kept his eye on the flames. They were closer now, and the smell of burning wood stung his nostrils. "Everyone to me," he said, spinning in place to see his men. His eye watched Ward and Carter walk over to him. They avoided the large carcass that was already rotting.

Around them, the jungle burned. Trees crackled and sputtered as it sucked the moisture from the bark. Branches covered in leaves erupted into flames, then after a second fell to the floor with a crash.

The fire ate everything, and the billowing smoke made it hard for the men to see and breathe.

"Sound off!" Armitage bellowed over the roar of the fire. He turned, struggling to see anything over the smoke, and each breath stung his lungs. "Goggles on," he added while he pulled up the spec-ops issued tactical goggles. The moment his eyes were covered, the tears vanished and he could see better. All he had to do now was figure out how to breathe and where his men were.

"Sound the fuck off!" he said again before dropping into a crouch. His vision was clearer, but the destruction before him didn't instill a sense of confidence. "Where's that helo?" he muttered as heavy footsteps approached from behind him.

"Calm your tits," Carter's voice came through loud over the comms. "Chuckie and I are fine and dandy," the two men dropped to the ground on either side of the team leader. "Ain't we, Chuck."

The medic nodded, then coughed loudly. "If we don't move soon enough, the smoke'll kill us all," Ward said as he pulled an SCBA over his face. Tapping the shield covering his face, the medic said, "This'll work better than goggles."

Carter and Armitage looked at each other, then to the medic. Ward's expression was one of disbelief and disappointment. "Put on the fucking masks!"

"You heard the man," Henry Armitage said with a small chuckle as he quickly removed the goggles and slipped on his own breathing gear. Instantly everything was easier and his mind focused. "Any sign of Sammy? Or Galindo?"

Before either man could answer, one tree groaned before it came tumbling down. The screech of wood snapping and breaking startled the three men who rolled out of the way.

The fiery trunk crashed down on top of the scorpion's carcass. The force of the impact caused the exoskeleton to crack, then explode. Blood, organs, juices and the stinger's venom erupted in a glorious fountain of viscera.

A moment later, the mixture of liquids made contact with the flames, and it ignited.

The explosion sucked the air and flames in before pushing it out. A deafening roar filled the air and the three men covered their heads, protecting them from any falling debris.

"We've got to get the fuck out of here!" Carter said as the flames grew closer and closer. The heat was unbearable and the three men felt drier than the Sahara. "I'm not going to burn!"

Armitage got to his knees and growled at the Captain,

"Nobody is going to burn! Look!" he pointed and the two men turned their heads, following the finger.

High above the raging fire, the men saw the smoke swirl and dance as rotor blades cut the air. Below the sounds of burning wood, the men heard the familiar sounds of a T700-GE-701C engine working at maximum capacity.

"Fuck yeah, you bloody ripper!" Carter said as he scrambled to his feet.

Armitage tapped his comms twice then said, "Sam, come in. Repeat, Sam, do you copy? Helo is inbound and we need you and the package. Where the fuck are you?"

That was the question on everyone's mind. But the rate at which the fire was spreading, their chances of making it to the Black Hawk were growing slimmer and slimmer with each passing second. They knew that the longer they waited, the sooner the door would be closed.

"What do we do, boss?" Ward asked. His eyes were focused on the fire and his mind began calculating how long it would take for them to burn to death.

Carter stepped up and said, "Give me a SITREP first. How long will it take for us to die if we stand around here all day?" Looking at his best friend in the world, the Captain said, "Keep on Sammy. He's probably got Galindo and is safe."

Spinning to stare at the man, Armitage said, "He better fucking be or I'll march right into hell to beat the shit out of him."

"You and me both," Carter said, and even though his face was obscured by the plastic mask, the man's smile was visible. "Chuckie?"

The medic shook his head as he looked at his superior officers. "Best bet is about five minutes," he said, then tapped his breather. "These won't last much longer. Either we move or—"

"Hank!" Nightingale's voice crackled through their earpieces and the three men grinned. "I've got Galindo with me. But we've got a problem… Oi! What did I say? Get the fuck down! Yeah, we've got more of those fucking scorpions. Can you get to us?"

"Location?" Armitage said without hesitation. Quickly he checked his carbine; it was still empty. As were the rest of his clips. Looking up, he saw the others shake their heads. They were all out of ammo.

They heard Nightingale grunt, then the sound of his carbine firing. "We're about five hundred meters from your position," the communications officer said. "I've got eyes on the helo too, so you better move."

"Got it," Armitage said as he turned to Ward and Carter. He opened his mouth, then quickly closed it and lifted his hand.

Turning, the two men saw four scorpions trample the burning trees. Each one was already on fire and the tails were swinging about wildly with the stingers twitching and uncontrollably dribbling venom.

The four arachnids barrelled into each other without a care. Screeches of pain and agony came from them, and the three soldiers watched as the massive pincers lashed out at one another. Tearing away sections of hard shell, the bugs attacked each other in a frenzy.

"What the fuck?" Carter said as he raised then lowered his weapon in quick succession.

Charles Dexter Ward stepped forward, then coughed. "It's the fire. They've gone crazy from the fire… We can use this to our advantage!"

"Bloody beauty!" Armitage said as he watched the stingers dive. Each stab caused an eruption of blood and the venom followed by a shriek from the wounded. "Sammy," the Major said into his comms while trying not to cough, "how many you got with you?"

Apart from the hiss of static, the comms were silent. The three men looked at one another, then to the brawling bugs. The flames were even closer to them now, and the heat was beyond unbearable.

"We need to go," Carter said while wiping his brow. "Fuck the bugs," he added as he tossed a grenade at the four scorpions.

CHAPTER TWENTY

The three men crashed through a wall of burning foliage. The bushes and branches broke easily around them leaving a path of destruction.

Ward shook his shoulders, casting off the burning twigs and flaming branches. "Can't see fucking shit," he said, sticking a finger inside the SCBA and wiping the film of condensation away. "Can we get the flying fuck out of here?"

Carter nodded, letting his M4A1 hang at his side as he pulled out his Kimber handgun. "At least we have the helo," he said happily.

Hovering above the inferno, the Black Hawk bobbed and weaved, doing its best to avoid taking unnecessary damage. Apart from the pilot and copilot sitting on either side manning M240 machine guns were two gunners.

"You fly-boys are a sight for sore eyes!" Armitage said as he waved at the helicopter.

A second later the earpieces crackled, and the pilot said, "Don't thank us yet. Your men are fucked and we can't get close enough yet."

"Shit," Carter said, suddenly remembering Nightingale and Galindo. "Sammy! Where the fuck are you?"

He needn't have asked as the giant screamed before hitting the ground. Galindo followed as the branch the two men were perched on gave way under the combined weight.

"You said they were fucked!?" Carter said while Armitage and Ward saw to the two fallen men.

The pilot spoke fast as the helicopter began its descent, "One man's 'fucked' is another's bad day."

"That's all we fucking need," Armitage said, shaking his head, "a philosophical pilot."

A chuckle filled their ears, and the pilot said, "If you'd rather wait for a more Chuck Yeager-type, just say the word." The flight crew laughed, and the gunners gave each other fist-bumps.

Below the helicopter, Armitage opened his mouth but Carter spoke, cutting him off. "Play nice, boys," the Captain said. His eyes scanned the wrecked trees. The flames were higher than before, and the smoke thicker than syrup. Looking down at Nightingale and Galindo he said, "Wake 'em up. Now!"

Armitage glanced at his second-in-command then said, "When did you take charge?"

The Captain said nothing as he spoke to the pilot, "Listen up! You need to get as low as possible but DO NOT FUCKING LAND!" Turning to his brothers, he said, "No fuck-ups. We—"

"We've got something on the radar," the copilot's voice was hesitant as he spoke. "Coming in fast too… They're not ours, right?"

Getting to his feet, Armitage said, "Keep an eye on it. Whatever it is, those M2s you've got will take care of anything thrown at you. Now, fucking get down here!"

Nightingale groaned, rolled his head from side to side, then opened his eyes. "Fuck this shit," he said weakly. "I'm ready to go home."

"Testify!" Ward said, laughing as the Black Hawk hovered a meter above the scorched earth.

Around the men and the aircraft, the trees swayed and bent dangerously. The structural integrity of their trunks destroyed by the fire, they were ready to fall and crush anything unlucky enough to be caught.

"Hurry the fuck up!" one gunner said, holding out a hand,

ready to help the men into the aircraft's hold.

The Cutthroats scrambled into the cargo hold and strapped themselves into place. Each member of the team smiled and gave each other celebratory high-fives before holding on as the aircraft lifted itself into the air.

Jorge Galindo moaned but didn't open his eyes. A large jagged gash ran across his face and the blood had already begun to congeal. He lay on a stretcher, arms and legs strapped down tight. He looked at peace but Ward pointed his weapon at the man.

"Patch me through to Carpenter," Armitage said the moment they had cleared the tree lines. Below, the men could see the true extent of the fire devouring a massive section of the Lacandon Jungle. Enormous plumes of black smoke billowed high into the sky, and the flocks of birds took flight as their nests were destroyed.

In front of the Major the copilot nodded, then said, "You guys look like shit." Nods of agreement came from the rest of the flight crew.

Carter flipped them off, then looked at Nightingale and Ward. The two soldiers sat there, sighing and holding in their emotions. Both sets of lips quivered as they relived the past day, the excruciating pain of losing both Gilman and Muldoon and the fact they'd almost died at the hands of humongous insects. Their eyes stared out at the expanse of green, then they hugged.

Both men were silent as they ended the hug, but their body language said it all; the team was empty.

"John!" Armitage said as his eyes focused on a series of black dots approaching them. "We're inbound with the package intact."

"Good man," General Carpenter's voice was beyond pleased. "Get back ASAP for some cold ones and that well-deserved vacation."

Armitage sighed. All he wanted was to rest and have his eye looked at. Since they'd had to swim in the river, it'd been itching and sending shots of intense pain straight to his brain and he was jacked with it.

"Anything else?"

"Yes, there is," Armitage answered Carpenter's question. "Rain hellfire on this place."

"Already done," Carpenter chuckled before static took over.

The gunner sitting closest to Carter squinted behind his sunglasses then said, "The fuck?" He raised a hand to point before screaming in pain as a mosquito's large tube-sucker impaled his torso. Blood erupted from his mouth and his body spasmed.

The other gunner screamed as the insect ripped his friend from his position. Loud snaps echoed as the safety-harness broke and the soldier vanished into the air.

"Evasive maneuvers!" the pilot shouted as he and the copilot began pulling on the control-sticks and pressing the pedals rapidly.

The younger man turned and added, "Hold on to your butts!" He grunted against the force of the engine working overtime. "We're under attack!"

Carter grunted, then growled. "No shit, Sherlock!" he said before reaching over and grabbing the gunner-less machine gun. Peering down the barrel, the constant bouncing made it almost impossible to get a clear shot at the attacking bugs. "Keep it fucking steady!"

Surrounding the Black Hawk, the seven mosquitoes bobbed and weaved, trying to get into the best position to attack.

Inside the aircraft, the men aimed the M240s, pulled back on the slide, then fired. The roar of the .50 calibre bullets leaving the barrels was almost drowned out by the rotor blades straining to keep the helicopter in front of the bugs.

"Are those fucking mosquitoes?" the pilot asked as he did everything to keep the bugs out of the hold. His brow furrowed. The man struggled to see past the sweat pouring from his hairline.

One of the flying menaces got too close to the spinning blades. Its fragile wings fluttered then were pulled back from the updraft and in an instant, the bug was sucked up into the rotor blades.

The 16.36 meter long metal blades shredded the insect in a glorious fountain of blood and bodily fluids that splattered the windshield. The pieces of flesh rained down onto the forest below.

A loud bang was heard, then smoke escaped from the fuselage.

"Fuck me sideways!" the copilot said as alarms blared and the control-stick rattled.

The pilot turned back to the group of men and said, "Hang on! We're going to have a—" his voice failed him as more and more mosquitoes appeared, dotting the sky with their elongated black bodies.

Carter and the other gunner continued to fire. The guns blazed, bullets shredding the bodies and wings of the bugs. But it was no use. The moment they ran out of ammunition, it was game over. It seemed like the insects were playing with the men, enjoying the thrill of the hunt before descending on them and feasting.

"Any ideas?" the Captain asked Armitage.

Henry Armitage smiled, then raised his hand. His thumb and index finger were in the shape of a gun, and the man imitated firing.

At once the mosquitoes exploded as 20mm rounds eviscerated them.

The roar of fighter jets sent a cheer through the men as three F-16 Fighting Falcons sped past the helicopter, circled around and performed another attack run.

The bugs turned and made for the intruders.

"You're clear," the lead jet's pilot said. "Proceed back to base. We've got you covered."

The Cutthroats cheered as the jets continued to fire at the mosquitoes. Each volley from their Gatling guns wiped out more of the flying insects in a mist of crimson and body parts.

"Enjoy the show," the lead pilot said with a small smile to his voice. "Payloads away."

The three F-16s launched their supply of AGM-114 Hellfire missiles. For a second they hung in the air before the jet engine took over and they sped towards their intended target.

"I love this part," Carter said with an enormous smile as the jets disappeared behind the clouds and the Hellfire missiles dipped before they vanished into the trees.

A second later, a series of explosions went off and the Valley of Bicho was engulfed in a spectacular fireball of destruction. A shockwave rocked the trees, then fire wiped out the rest in one clean strike.

As the Black Hawk continued its journey back to base camp,

The Cutthroats nodded at each other and enjoyed the rampant destruction. Slowly, each one closed their eyes as they realised the ordeal and mission was over.

CHAPTER TWENTY-ONE

"Sir," Armitage said with a wince. His legs still ached and the cane they'd given him was of little help. In his mind they might as well have given him a corn husk to lean on. He still didn't know how he had survived. But one thing was clear, The Cutthroats would fight another day.

All but one of the Generals were deep in conversation, their entire focus on the files each one held. Cold beads of sweat danced on their foreheads and it was obvious they didn't know what to make of the official report.

General Carpenter appeared calm, cool and collected. His eyes didn't bother with the files. In fact, they were discarded on his large impressive desk. Instead, the pale blue eyes were focused just on Armitage. "Yes, what is it, Henry?"

Like always, Armitage felt like the only man in the room when Carpenter spoke to him. The other Generals were still busy in their own argument, but at the sound of Carpenter's voice they stopped talking and looked up at the weary looking, one-eyed Commander. Armitage straightened somewhat under the stares.

"Relax, Hank," Carpenter said with a slight chuckle. "No need to stand on formalities," his eyes went to a blonde General. "Albert, get a chair for our guest."

The General blinked. It had been a long time since anyone had given him an order, and the feeling was strange. "Beg pardon?"

Carpenter quickly winked at Armitage before speaking. "You heard me," he said. "Henry here is still recuperating. Any second now he's going to collapse. Be a good lad and get him one."

The other Generals chuckled. Nobody liked the blonde man, so it was good to see him being put to the test. Carpenter was the highest-ranking man in the room, it was his office the meeting was happening in, and nobody messed with him.

The blonde General nodded and quickly pulled a large comfy looking chair over to Armitage. "Thank you, Sir," he said with a polite nod, "but I prefer to stand."

Carpenter raised a hand as if to say, 'Not a problem' to the man. "As you wish," he said. "What is it, Henry?"

Armitage cleared his throat, the pain in his right eye… no, the bloody pulpy mess that until recently held his eye… wept blood and felt itchy. The doctors had tried their best, but all they could do was give him an eye-patch and tell him to clean it twice a week. He wanted to scratch it, but his discipline from training kept his hands clenched to his sides.

"Sir, is there a problem with my report?" he asked, trying to make his voice sound complacent. The last thing he needed or wanted was for Carpenter to think he was aiming for a fight. Right now, he needed them to pay for his treatments and keep him working.

Carpenter shook his head, "Not at all!" He smiled at the man, "But we did have some suggestions for you. It's nothing major, just a few things to make everything easier and avoid unnecessary questions being asked… You understand?"

On a level, Armitage did. But right now, the former Team Leader for The Cutthroats wanted the world, or at least the Brass to know about what they found in Mexico. "I'm not sure I do," he said without thinking.

"Henry," another of the Generals said, his tone warning, "take care with how you speak to us—"

"Let him be," Carpenter said. "He's had a rough time losing most of his team like that. Dreadful business." He sighed, then said while staring directly at Armitage, "But those are the risks when dealing with the cartels. Am I right?"

Henry Armitage knew exactly what the General meant. But it contradicted the report he had filed the day before. "Sir," he said slowly, "yes. The cartels do pose a risk to any team sent in with the sole purpose of capturing one leader. But we didn't do that."

"That's not what this document says," the older man said, holding up an already formatted and signed piece of paper. Carpenter read the letter, mumbling under his breath the words to great effect. The other Generals looked bored by the performance. "Ah!" he exclaimed when he reached the pertinent part. "Here it is. Team designated as 'The Cutthroats' proceeded with the operation as specified by General Carpenter. Unfortunately, local intelligence proved too untrustworthy and the number of men under the control of Jorge Galindo was more than given. This proved to be the deciding factor in the mission's failure."

Armitage opened his mouth to protest. He couldn't believe what he was hearing. The new report was a complete fabrication, and it sounded like he would be given the blame. Carpenter ignored the opened mouth and continued reading out loud, "Only Team Leader Henry Armitage, Captain Randolph Carter, Specialists Charles Dexter Ward and Sam Nightingale got out alive, whereas the rest of the team were KIA by the hired army of Galindo. After air-support was dispatched and the team recovered, AGM-114 Hellfire missiles were used to clear the hot-spot. Once this was accomplished, a recon team was dispatched to confirm that the target was eliminated, and the mission was deemed a success with TL Armitage being awarded honours."

The Generals stared at Armitage, gauging his expression and reaction to the new narrative.

His mind raced, trying to figure what reason the old men would have to rewrite what happened to his team. It seemed like they were disrespecting the memory of his brothers-in-arms. For Armitage it wouldn't do. Not at all.

"Well, Henry," Carpenter said, "what do you think?"

A second was all it took for him to put his thoughts together. "With all due respect, Sir," Armitage began, "I think that lie you have concocted is a slap in the face of my men. What we encountered was beyond anything thought possible, or real. For fuck's sake, even with a proper briefing, I seriously doubt we would have survived. I am grateful for you to give me an award. But what about the rest of my team? And Galindo. What is going to happen to him? He's still alive. I know that for a fact."

The other Generals looked at each other. Their faces wore a mixture of blank indifference and slight confusion. They looked to Carpenter whose face was the perfect picture of calm serenity. "The Cutthroats will be given their just rewards. We don't mention it here because the Brass don't care about the dead. But I give you my word we will take care of the families."

"And Galindo?"

Now it was Carpenter's turn to look confused. His eyes darted to the files splayed all over his desk and they skimmed the printed words and he frowned. "Henry," he said slowly, "are you sure you're feeling fine and should be up and about?"

Armitage nodded.

"Fair enough… I only ask because… well, to be frank, we don't have any record of Jorge Galindo being brought in," Carpenter sounded less than convinced of his own words.

"What?" Armitage asked as his world crumbled. "I put him into the Black Hawk that brought us back here! My men, Carter and Ward, took him to medical for an inspection. Jorge Galindo is alive and somewhere here."

"Yes," the blonde General said with a grave nod of his head, "your report made that quite clear. But, Henry, there are no records of Galindo being brought in, dead or alive. You didn't find him. We did, his body was among the dead left after the Hellfire strike." He frowned then asked, "Maybe your memory was rattled when you lost that eye?"

"Don't speak to me… Sir," Armitage said softly. It was a tone of voice that all men knew instantly, and it said only one thing. This man was dangerous and should not be pissed off. "General," he said, turning to Carpenter, "my report is sound—"

"Henry," Carpenter's stern voice stopped the man clean in his tracks. "We're not doubting your words. Not at all. If you say that Jorge Galindo was with you, then he was. What we are saying is that our records show no person of that name having been brought in alive. And for the good of us all, it should remain that way."

His meaning became clear, and in that moment, Henry Armitage knew exactly what was happening. Galindo was now lost in the system and most likely would be used as a source of intelligence for other operations. He hated the idea, but this was the truth.

He had heard about this happening before to other teams. And on some level he was okay with it. "Sir," he said with just the tiniest hint of a smile, "I am more than happy to sign your report here and now."

The smile Carpenter returned was one of gratitude. "Soon Hank," he said, "for now I need you to rest and get your strength back."

"May I ask why?"

"I'd be worried if you didn't," the General said with a laugh. "We've got a mission that needs just the right touch. And you're the man with the golden touch. So, get some R&R and then once the medics give you a clean bill of health, organise a new team. You got that, soldier?"

"Sir, yessir!"

THE END

SEVERED**PRESS**

facebook.com/severedpress
twitter.com/severedpress

CHECK OUT OTHER GREAT HORROR NOVELS

BLACK FRIDAY
by Michael Hodges

Jared the kleptomaniac, Chike the unemployed IT guy, Patricia the shopaholic, and Jeff the meth dealer are trapped inside a Chicago supermall on Black Friday. Bridgefield Mall empties during a fire alarm, and most of the shoppers drive off into a strange mist surrounding the mall parking lot. They never return. Chike and his group try calling friends and family, but their smart phones won't work, not even Twitter. As the mist creeps closer, the mall lights flicker and surge. Bulbs shatter and spray glass into the air. Unsettling noises are heard from within the mist, as the meth dealer becomes unhinged and hunts the group within the mall. Cornered by the mist, and hunted from within, Chike and the survivors must fight for their lives while solving the mystery of what happened to Bridgefield Mall. Sometimes, a good sale just isn't worth it.

GRIMWEAVE
by Tim Curran

In the deepest, darkest jungles of Indochina, an ancient evil is waiting in a forgotten, primeval valley. It is patient, monstrous, and bloodthirsty. Perfectly adapted to its hot, steaming environment, it strikes silent and stealthy, it chosen prey: human. Now Michael Spiers, a Marine sniper, the only survivor of a previous encounter with the beast, is going after it again. Against his better judgement, he is made part of a Marine Force Recon team that will hunt it down and destroy it.

The hunters are about to become the hunted.

Printed in Great Britain
by Amazon

79613929R00078